PUFFIN BOOKS

LOTTIE AND LISA

Lottie and Lisa were strangers when they met at a summer school. Yet they looked exactly alike, although Lisa had fair curls, and Lottie had two fair plaits. When they became friends they discovered that they were twin sisters although one lived with her father in Vienna and the other with her mother in Munich, and their parents never talked about each other. So they hatched a daring plan to exchange homes: jotting down the elaborate details of each other's lives in exercise books. But *could* Lisa ever learn to cook as well as Lottie? Would Lottie succeed in being as gay and lively as Lisa, could she ever eat as many stuffed pancakes as Lisa was known to enjoy? Would the letters addressed to 'Forget-me-not' arrive in time to answer frantic questions? You must discover the answers in the book itself, but we promise you that the twins had a wonderful time, and so will you as you share their anxieties and pleasures.

Erich Kästner was born in Dresden in 1899 and went straight from school to fight in the First World War. In order to go to university he worked in his spare time as a journalist, but some of his articles caused trouble and at twenty-eight he was dismissed. He went to Berlin to try his luck as a writer, and within a year had published his first book. Others followed, and *Emil and the Detectives* was filmed, dramatized and translated into twenty-five languages. Then in 1933, Hitler came to power, and Kästner's books were publicly burned with those of twenty-three other authors. He stayed in Germany but for the next twelve years his books were banned. After the war he worked for a newspaper in Munich. He died in 1974.

D1421620

Some other books by Erich Kästner

**EMIL AND THE DETECTIVES
EMIL AND THE THREE TWINS
THE FLYING CLASSROOM
THE LITTLE MAN**

ERICH KÄSTNER

Lottie and Lisa

TRANSLATED BY CYRUS BROOKS

Illustrated by Walter Trier

PUFFIN BOOKS
in association with Jonathan Cape

PUFFIN BOOKS

Published by the Penguin Group
Penguin Books Ltd, 27 Wrights Lane, London W8 5TZ, England
Penguin Books USA Inc., 375 Hudson Street, New York, New York 10014, USA
Penguin Books Australia Ltd, Ringwood, Victoria, Australia
Penguin Books Canada Ltd, 10 Alcorn Avenue, Toronto, Ontario, Canada M4V 3B2
Penguin Books (NZ) Ltd, 182–190 Wairau Road, Auckland 10, New Zealand

Penguin Books Ltd, Registered Offices: Harmondsworth, Middlesex, England

First published in Germany 1949
Published in Great Britain by Jonathan Cape 1950
Published in Puffin Books 1962
19 20 18

Printed in England by Clays Ltd, St Ives plc
Set in Monotype Times Roman

Chapter 1

Do you happen to know Bohrlaken? I mean the village in the mountains – Bohrlaken on Lake Bohren? No? You don't? Odd – none of the people I ask seems to know Bohrlaken. Maybe Bohrlaken is one of those places known only to the people I *don't* ask. It wouldn't surprise me. Such things do happen.

Well, if you don't know Bohrlaken on Lake Bohren, then of course you don't know the holiday home at Bohrlaken on Lake Bohren either, the well-known holiday home for little girls. Pity. But never mind. Children's holiday homes are as alike as peas in a pod; if you know one you know them all. And if you happened to stroll past one you might think it was a giant beehive. Such a hum of shouts, laughs, giggles, and whispers. These holiday homes are beehives of happiness and high spirits. And however many there may be, there can never be enough of them.

Though sometimes of an evening, of course, the grey dwarf Homesickness sits by the beds in the dormitories, takes from his pocket his grey notebook and his grey pencil and with a glum face counts up the tears around him, those shed and those unshed.

But next morning – hey presto! – he's vanished. Then the milk cups chink and the little tongues chatter for all they're worth. Then swarms of bathing-caps race again into the cool, bottle-green lake, splash, scream, yelp, crow, swim – or at least pretend to be swimming.

*

That's how it is at Bohrlaken on Lake Bohren, where the story begins which I am going to tell you. It's a rather complicated story. And now and then you'll have to pay careful attention if you are really going to get the hang of it all. It's quite straightforward at the beginning; it doesn't begin to get complicated till later on. Complicated and pretty thrilling.

Well, now they are all bathing in the lake, and the one that is playing the maddest pranks is, as usual, a little girl of nine with a head framed in curls and filled with bright ideas, whose name is Lisa, Lisa Palfy. From Vienna.

A gong booms from the house. One, two, three. The children and the young lady helpers who are still bathing clamber up the bank.

6

'That means all of you,' called Miss Ulrica. 'Including Lisa.'

'I'm coming,' cried Lisa. 'I'm not jet-propelled!' And then she came.

Miss Ulrica drove her cackling flock into the pen – I beg your pardon – into the house. At twelve sharp they had lunch. And then they waited, looking forward eagerly to the afternoon. Why?

That afternoon twenty new girls were arriving. Twenty little girls from South Germany. Would there be a few dressed-up dollies among them? A few chatterboxes? Or would they be a lot of old dames of thirteen or fourteen? Would they bring some decent toys? With good luck there might be a large rubber ball. Trudie's had no air in it. Brigit had one, but she wouldn't bring it out. She had shut it up in her locker. And locked it. In case of accidents. Such things do happen.

*

So that afternoon Lisa, Trudie, Brigit, and the others stood around the big, wide-open, iron gates, waiting impatiently for the bus which would bring the new girls from the nearest railway station. If the train came in on time, they ought to be –

A car hooted. 'They're coming!' The bus came speeding up the road, turned cautiously through the gates, and came to a stop. The driver got down and lifted the little girls, one after the other, out of the bus. But not only the girls – also the trunks, cases, dolls, baskets, paper bags, woolly dogs, parcels, umbrellas, thermos-flasks, mackintoshes, rucksacks, rolled-up rugs, picture-books, specimen-cases, and butterfly-nets – a gaudy jumble of baggage.

And finally the twentieth little girl appeared with her belongings in the framework of the door. A grave, demure little thing. The driver held out his hands.

Lisa and the new girl were the living spit of each other

The little girl shook her head, and as she did so her two plaits flew out behind.

'No, thank you,' she said, firmly and politely, and climbed down, calm and self-assured, from the step. She looked round with a shy smile, and suddenly her eyes opened wide with surprise. She had caught sight of Lisa. Then Lisa's eyes opened wide too as she looked with a startled expression into the new girl's face.

The other girls and Miss Ulrica stared in perplexity from one to the other. The driver pushed back his cap, scratched his head, and forgot to shut his mouth. But why?

Lisa and the new girl were the living spit of each other. It is true that one had long curls and the other tightly braided plaits – but that was really the sole difference between them!

Lisa turned and ran into the garden as though pursued by lions and tigers.

'Lisa!' cried Miss Ulrica. 'Lisa!' Then she shrugged her shoulders and turned to shepherd the twenty new girls into the house. And the last to follow, uncertain and infinitely surprised, was the girl with the plaits.

*

Mrs Mutesius, the head supervisor of the holiday home, was seated in her office, discussing with the rugged old cook the menu for the next few days.

There was a knock. Miss Ulrica came in and announced that the correct number of new girls had arrived safe and sound.

'Very good. Thank you.'

'There's something else –'

'Yes?' The overworked head looked up quickly.

'It's about Lisa Palfy,' began Miss Ulrica doubtfully. 'She's waiting outside the door –'

'Bring the little monkey in.' Mrs Mutesius could not suppress a smile. 'What mischief has she been up to now?'

'Nothing this time,' said Miss Ulrica. 'It's only –'

9

She opened the door cautiously and called: 'Come in, both of you! Don't be afraid!'

The two girls entered the room and stopped – a long way apart from each other.

'God bless my soul!' exclaimed the cook.

Mrs Mutesius shrugged her shoulders

Mrs Mutesius simply stared at the two children in bewilderment, so Miss Ulrica went on: 'The new girl is called Lottie Horn and comes from Munich.'

'Are you related to each other?'

The two girls shook their heads, unnoticeably but with conviction.

'They'd never set eyes on each other until today,' said Miss Ulrica. 'Curious, isn't it?'

'How is it curious,' asked the cook. 'How could they have set eyes on each other when the one comes from Munich and the other from Vienna?'

Mrs Mutesius said in a friendly voice: 'Two girls who look so alike are sure to be good friends. Don't stand so far apart. Come, children! Shake hands with each other.'

'No!' cried Lisa, and folded her arms behind her back.

Mrs Mutesius shrugged her shoulders, thought for a moment, and then said, 'You can both go.'

Lisa ran to the door, wrenched it open, and dashed out. Lottie dropped a curtsey and turned sedately to leave the room.

'Just a moment, Lottie,' said the head. She opened a big book. 'I'll enter your name at once. And when and where you were born. And your parents' names.'

'I've only got my Mummy,' said Lottie softly.

Mrs Mutesius dipped her pen in the inkpot. 'First, date of birth?'

*

Lottie walked down the corridor, went up the stairs, opened a door, and entered the locker-room. Her trunk was not yet unpacked. She began putting her frocks, slips, pinafores, and stockings into the locker assigned to her. Children's far-off laughter came in through the open window.

Lottie was holding in her hand the photograph of a young woman. She looked at it lovingly and then laid it carefully under her pinafores. When she came to close the locker, her eyes fell on a mirror on the

11

Lisa was sitting on the garden wall with her friends

inside of the door. She examined her own face gravely and searchingiy, as though she were seeing it for the first time. Then, with a sudden impulse, she threw back her plaits and arranged her hair on the top of her head so that it looked like Lisa Palfy's.

Somewhere a door slammed. Lottie dropped her hands as though she had been caught doing something wrong.

*

Lisa was sitting on the garden-wall with her friends; her brows were puckered in a frown.

'*I* wouldn't stand for it,' said Trudie, a school-fellow from Vienna. 'The cheek of it – coming here with your face!'

'Well, what can I do?' asked Lisa angrily.

'Scratch it for her,' suggested Monica.

'The best thing is to bite her nose off,' advised Christine. 'Then you've got rid of the cause of the trouble at one go!' She swung her legs light-heartedly as she spoke.

'Messing up my holidays like this,' muttered Lisa, embittered.

'But she can't help it,' remarked chubby-faced Steffie. 'If somebody came and looked like *me*, I –'

Trudie laughed. 'Surely you don't think anybody would be such a chump as to go around looking like you!'

Steffie sulked. The others laughed. Even Lisa smiled a little.

Then the gong sounded.

'Feeding time for the wild animals!' cried Christine. And the girls jumped down from the wall.

*

Mrs Mutesius remarked to Miss Ulrica in the dining-hall: 'We'll take the bull by the horns and let those two doubles sit together.'

The children came streaming noisily into the hall. There was a scraping of chair-legs. The girls on duty carried steaming tureens to the tables, and others filled the plates eagerly held out to them.

Miss Ulrica came up behind Lisa and Trudie and tapped Trudie lightly on the shoulder. 'You are to sit by Hilda Storm,' she said.

Trudie turned and was about to say something. 'But –'

'No objections, please.'

13

Trudie shrugged her shoulders, got up, pouted, and walked away.

Spoons clattered. The chair next to Lisa's was empty. It is amazing how much attention an empty chair can attract.

Then, as though at a word of command, all eyes turned to the door. Lottie had just come in.

'Here you are at last,' said Miss Ulrica. 'Come along. I'll show you your place.' She led the grave, demure little girl with the plaits towards the table. Lisa did not look up; she went on furiously spooning her soup. Lottie sat down obediently beside Lisa and took up her spoon, though she felt as though her throat were tied up with a piece of string.

The other girls, fascinated, squinted over at the unusual pair. A calf with two, or even three, heads could not have excited more curiosity. Plump, chubby-faced Steffie was so thrilled that she forgot to shut her mouth.

Lisa could control her feelings no longer. And, what's more, she didn't want to. With all her strength she kicked out under the table at Lottie's shin.

Lottie winced with pain, and pressed her lips firmly together.

*

At the grown-ups' table Miss Gerda, one of the helpers, shook her head and remarked, 'I can't make it out – two absolute strangers and such a remarkable resemblance!'

Miss Ulrica said thoughtfully, 'Perhaps they're astrological twins.'

14

'What on earth is that?' asked Miss Gerda. 'Astrological twins?'

'I've heard there are people who are absolutely identical in appearance without being even distantly related. They happen to have been born in the same fraction of the same second.'

'Oh!' murmured Miss Gerda.

Mrs Mutesius nodded. 'I remember reading of a

A tailor who looked like King Edward VII

tailor in London who looked exactly like King Edward VII. You couldn't tell them apart. Especially as the tailor wore the same kind of pointed beard as the king. King Edward summoned him to Buckingham Palace and had a long talk with him.'

'And they had actually been born in the same second?'

'Yes. By chance they were able to verify it exactly.'

'And what happened after that?' asked Miss Gerda, deeply interested.

'By the king's wish the tailor shaved off his beard.'

While the others were laughing, Mrs Mutesius looked reflectively across to the table where the two girls were sitting. 'We'd better give Lottie Horn the bed next to Lisa Palfy,' she said. 'They'll have to get used to each other.'

*

It was night. All the children were asleep. Except two.

These two had turned their backs on each other and pretended to be fast asleep. But they were lying with eyes wide open, staring into the moonlit room.

Lisa looked crossly at the odd-shaped silver patch the moon had made on her bed. Suddenly she pricked up her ears. She heard someone crying, quietly, fitfully.

Lottie pressed her hands to her mouth. What was it her mother had said when she left? – 'I'm so glad you're going to spend a few weeks with all those happy children. You are too serious for your age, Lottie. Much too serious. I know it's not your fault, but mine. It's because of my work. I'm away from home too much. And when I do get home, I'm tired. And then you've not been playing like other children, but washing up, cooking, and laying the table. See that you come back home with a lot of smile-wrinkles, my little housekeeper!' And now she was lying here in a strange room, next to a bad-tempered girl who hated her because she happened to look like her. She sighed softly. And she was to get smile-wrinkles! Lottie began to sob quietly to herself.

Suddenly she felt a little strange hand awkwardly stroking her hair.

Lottie stiffened with fright. With fright? Lisa's hand went on shyly stroking her hair.

The moon looked in through the big dormitory window and was surprised at what it saw – two little girls lying side by side, not daring to look at each other. And the one, who had just been crying, slowly putting out her hand and feeling for the other's hand as it stroked her hair.

'Well, well,' thought the old silver moon. 'Now I can go down with a clear conscience.'

Which it did.

Chapter 2

WAS it a real armistice between those two? Would it last? – Although it had been made without negotiation, without even a word? Yes, I think so. But it's a long way from an armistice to peace. Even among children. Or, is it?

They did not dare look at each other next morning when they woke up; nor when they ran in their long white nightgowns to the wash-room; nor when they dressed at neighbouring lockers; nor when, on neighbouring chairs, they drank their breakfast milk; not even when they ran side by side along the lake-shore and, later, danced round-dances with the helpers and made daisy-chains. Only once did their eyes meet in a quick, fleeting glance, and then, frightened, they looked quickly away again.

Now Miss Ulrica was sitting in a meadow, reading a wonderful novel which had something about love on every page. Now and then she lowered the book and her mind went far away as she thought of Mr Rademacher, the engineer who lodged with her aunt. His name was Rudolf. Oh, Rudolf!

Meanwhile Lisa was playing ball with her friends. But her thoughts were not on the game. Often she looked round as though searching for someone who was not there.

Trudie asked, 'When are you going to bite the new girl's nose off, eh?'

Miss Ulrica was sitting in a meadow, reading

'Don't be such an idiot!' snapped Lisa.

Christine looked at her in surprise. 'Hello! I thought you were mad with her?'

'I can't bite off everybody's nose when I'm mad with them,' returned Lisa coldly. And she added, 'Besides, I'm *not* mad with her.'

'But you were yesterday,' insisted Steffie.

'And how!' said Monica. 'At supper you gave her such a kick under the table that she nearly yelled.'

'You see?' said Trudie with evident satisfaction.

Lisa bristled. 'If you don't shut up at once,' she

19

cried fiercely, '*you'll* get a kick on the shins!' And with that she turned and ran off.

'She doesn't know what she wants,' remarked Christine, shrugging her shoulders.

*

Lottie was sitting alone in the meadow. On the top of her head was a little chaplet of flowers, and she was busily engaged in making another. Suddenly a shadow fell across her pinafore. She looked up.

The two doubles were sitting side by side on the grass

Lisa was there in front of her, hopping from one foot to the other, uncertain and embarrassed.

Lottie risked a little smile. Hardly big enough to see, except with a magnifying glass.

Lisa smiled back, relieved.

Lottie held up the flower-chain she had just completed, and asked shyly, 'Would you like it?'

Lisa dropped on one knee and said passionately, 'Yes, but only if you put it on.'

Lottie placed the flowers on her curls. Then she nodded. 'Lovely,' she said.

Now the two doubles were sitting side by side on the grass, all alone, finding nothing to say, but smiling warily at each other.

Then Lisa took a deep breath and asked, 'Are you still angry with me?'

Lottie shook her head.

Lisa looked at the ground. 'It was so sudden,' she said, forcing out the words. 'The bus! And then *you*! Such a shock!'

Lottie nodded. 'Such a shock,' she repeated.

Lisa leant forward. 'But really it's jolly good fun, isn't it?'

Surprised, Lottie looked into her bright, merry eyes.

'Fun?' Then she asked softly, 'Have you any brothers and sisters?'

'No.'

'Nor me,' said Lottie.

*

The two girls had slipped away to the wash-room and were standing in front of a large mirror. Lottie, keen as mustard, was tugging with brush and comb at Lisa's curls.

Lisa cried, 'Oh!' and 'Ah-uh!'

21

'Will you keep quiet?' scolded Lottie with pretended severity. 'Do you yell like that when your Mummy does your plaits?'

'I haven't got a Mummy,' muttered Lisa. 'That's why – Ah-uh! – that's why I'm such a little rowdy, Daddy says.'

'Doesn't he ever take a slipper to you?' inquired Lottie earnestly, as she began plaiting Lisa's hair.

'Not on your life. He's much too fond of me.'

'That has nothing to do with it,' observed Lottie very wisely.

'And besides he's got too many other things to do.'

'It only needs one hand.' Both laughed.

Then Lisa's plaits were finished, and the two girls looked with eager eyes into the mirror. Their faces shone like Christmas trees. Two absolutely identical girls looked into the mirror. Two absolutely identical girls looked back out of it.

'Like two sisters!' whispered Lottie warmly.

The midday gong sounded.

'This is going to be fun!' cried Lisa. 'Come on!' As they ran out of the wash-room, they were holding hands.

*

The other girls had taken their places long ago. Only Lisa's and Lottie's chairs were still unoccupied.

Then the door opened and Lottie appeared. Without hesitating she sat down in Lisa's place.

'I say,' warned Monica. 'That's Lisa's place. Look out for your shins.'

Lottie shrugged and began to eat.

The door opened again and – bless my soul! – Lottie, Lottie in the flesh, came in a second time. Without turning a hair she went to the last unoccupied seat and sat down.

The other girls at the table opened their eyes and mouths.

Those from the neighbouring tables stared across and then jumped up from their seats and crowded round the two Lotties.

The tension did not relax till the two girls burst out laughing. And inside a minute the hall was echoing with many-voiced, childish laughter.

Mrs Mutesius frowned sternly. 'What's all that noise about?' She rose and strode with ominous and regal steps into the thick of it. But when she saw both girls with plaits, her wrath melted like snow in the sun. She was quite amused as she asked, 'Now which of you is Lisa Palfy and which Lottie Horn?'

'We're not going to tell you,' said the one Lottie, with a twinkle, and the treble laughter burst out again.

'Well, for heaven's sake!' cried Mrs Mutesius in comical despair. 'What are we to do about it?'

'Perhaps,' suggested the second Lottie cheerfully, 'perhaps somebody can find out after all.'

Steffie waved her hand in the air as though she badly wanted to recite a poem: 'I know,' she cried. 'Trudie's in the same class as Lisa. Trudie must tell us.'

Trudie pushed her way doubtfully into the foreground, looked carefully from one Lottie to the other, and shook her head helplessly. But then a

23

roguish smile crossed her face. She took hold of one of the plaits of the nearest Lottie and gave it a sharp tug. Next moment came the noise of a hearty slap.

Holding her cheek, Trudie shouted triumphantly, 'That was Lisa!' (At which the general hilarity broke out louder than ever.)

*

Lisa and Lottie had been given permission to go down to the village. Their 'doubleness' was to be fixed for all time in a photograph. So that they could send home some prints. What a surprise for their parents!

After recovering from his first astonishment, the photographer, a certain Mr Appeldauer, made an excellent job of it. He took six different photographs. The postcards were to be ready in ten days.

When the two girls had gone, he said to his wife, 'D'you know what I shall do? – I shall send a few shiny prints to an illustrated paper or a magazine. Editors are often interested in things like that.'

Safely outside, Lisa was undoing her 'silly' plaits, for that sober hair-style imposed a certain strain upon her. When she could shake her curls freely she really felt she was herself again. She invited Lottie to a glass of lemonade. Lottie objected. Lisa said emphatically, 'You must! The day before yesterday Daddy sent me some more pocket-money. Come on!'

So they walked out to the house of the forester who kept a little café. They sat down at a table in the garden, drank lemonade, and talked. There is so much to say, so many questions to ask and answer, when two little girls have just made friends with each other.

The hens ran to and fro, pecking and clucking between the tables. An old retriever came up to sniff the two children, and found no objection to their remaining.

Mr Appeldauer took six different photographs

'Has your father been dead long?' asked Lisa.

'I don't know,' said Lottie. 'Mummy never mentions him and I don't like to ask.'

Lisa nodded. 'I can't remember my mother at all. There used to be a big photograph of her on Daddy's piano. But once he came in and caught me looking at it, and next day it was gone. I think he locked it up in his desk.'

The hens clucked. The retriever dozed. A little girl who had no father was drinking lemonade with a little girl who had no mother.

'You're nine too, aren't you?' asked Lisa.

'Yes,' Lottie nodded. 'I shall be ten on the fourteenth of October.'

Lisa sat up as straight as a poker. 'On the fourteenth of October?'

'On the fourteenth of October.'

Lisa leaned forward and whispered. 'So shall I!'

Lottie went as stiff as an icicle.

A cock crowed beyond the house. The retriever snapped at a bee that was buzzing round him. Through the open kitchen window they could hear the forester's wife singing.

The two girls looked into each other's eyes as though hypnotized. Lottie swallowed hard and asked, hoarse with excitement, 'And – *where* were you born?'

Lisa answered, in a low hesitant voice, as though she were afraid, 'At Linz on the Danube.'

Lottie moistened her dry lips with her tongue. 'So was I!'

In the garden all was still. Only the tips of the trees were moving. Perhaps Fate, gliding at that moment across the garden, touched them with its wing-tips.

Lottie said slowly, 'There's a photo of – of my Mummy in my locker.'

Lisa jumped up. 'Show it me!' She dragged Lottie from her chair and out of the garden.

'Hi!' shouted an injured voice. 'This is a nice way

of carrying on!' It was the forester's wife. 'Drinking lemonade and going off without paying!'

Lisa was shocked. With trembling fingers she rummaged in her purse, pressed a small and much crumpled note into the woman's hand, and ran back to Lottie.

'What about the change?' shouted the woman. But the two children did not hear. They were running as though for dear life.

'Now where are those young monkeys off to?' muttered the forester's wife. She went back into the house, and the old retriever trotted after her.

*

Back at the holiday home, Lottie hurriedly searched her locker. She found the photograph beneath a pile of clothes and held it out to Lisa, whose whole body was on the jump with eagerness.

Lisa took a shy, frightened look at the picture. Then her face brightened. Her eyes were firmly glued to a woman's face.

Lottie's face was turned expectantly towards Lisa.

Exhausted with sheer happiness, Lisa lowered the photograph and nodded blissfully. Then she hugged it passionately, and whispered, 'My Mummy!'

Lottie put her arm round Lisa's neck. '*Our* Mummy!' Two little girls clung tightly to each other. Behind the mystery that had just been solved for them, fresh mysteries, new problems, were waiting.

The gong rang through the house. Children ran laughing and shouting down the stairs. Lisa made a move to put the photograph back in the locker, but Lottie said, 'You can keep it.'

*

Miss Ulrica was standing before the desk in the head's office. She was so excited that on each of her cheeks was a round spot, red as a crab apple.

'I *can't* keep it to myself,' she blurted out. 'I *must* confide in you. If only I knew what we ought to do!'

'Come, come,' said Mrs Mutesius. 'What have you got on your mind, my dear?'

'They are *not* astrological twins.'

'Who aren't?' asked Mrs Mutesius with a smile. 'King Edward and the tailor?'

'No. Lisa Palfy and Lottie Horn! I've looked up the registration book. They were both born on the same day of the year at Linz. It simply *cannot* be a coincidence.'

'I don't think it's a coincidence either, my dear. In fact I have some ideas of my own on the subject.'

'So you know?' asked Miss Ulrica, panting for breath.

'Of course. When little Lottie arrived, I got her date and place of birth and entered them in the book. Then I compared them with Lisa's. That was the obvious thing to do, wasn't it?'

'Yes, yes. But what do we do now?'

'Nothing.'

'Nothing?'

'Nothing! Unless you keep it dark, I'll be furiously annoyed, my dear.'

'But –'

'There's no "but". The two children suspect nothing. They have just been photographed together and they'll send the prints home. If that helps to unravel the knot, well and good. But as for you and me, we'll take very good care not to play the role of fate. Thank you for your sympathetic understanding, my dear. And now, please send in cook to me.'

Miss Ulrica did not wear a particularly intelligent expression as she left the office. And, if she had, it would have been something quite unusual.

Chapter 3

TIME passed. It knows no better.

Have the two girls collected their photographs from Mr Appeldauer? Long ago. Did the inquisitive Miss Ulrica inquire whether they had sent home the prints? She did. Did Lisa and Lottie nod their heads and say yes? I fear so.

And those same prints, torn into little pieces, have been lying all the time at the bottom of bottle-green Lake Bohren near Bohrlaken. The two girls told Miss Ulrica a lie. They wanted to keep their secret to themselves. Together they wanted to hide it, and together, perhaps, reveal it. And they lied shamelessly to anyone who tried to pry too closely into their affairs. What else could they do? Their consciences did not prick them – not even Lottie's. And that is saying a good deal.

The two girls stuck together like burrs. Trudie, Steffie, Monica, Christine, and the rest were sometimes cross with Lisa and jealous of Lottie. What good did it do? None at all! Where had they slipped off to now?

*

They had slipped off to the locker-room. Lottie took two identical pinafores from her locker, gave one to her sister, and tied the other round herself.

'Mummy bought these,' she said, 'at Pollinger's.'

The two girls stuck together like burrs

'Aha,' exclaimed Lisa. 'That's the store in Neuhauser Street, near – What is the name of that gate?'

'Carl's Gate.'

'That's right – near Carl's Gate.'

By now they were mutually well-informed about each other's way of life, school-friends, neighbours, teachers, and flats. For Lisa everything connected with her mother was terribly important. And Lottie longed to know anything, any little thing, that her sister could tell her about her father. For days on end they talked of nothing else. And in bed at night they whispered together for hours. Each discovered a new and strange continent. What had been hitherto encompassed by their childhood's sky was, they suddenly realized, only half a world.

And at moments when they were not hard at work fitting together these two halves in order to get a glimpse of the whole, another subject excited them, another mystery tormented them: Why were their parents no longer together?

'First, of course, they got married,' explained Lisa for the hundredth time. 'Then they had us two. And they christened me Lisa and you Lottie because Mummy's name is Lisalotte. That's pretty, isn't it? They must have been fond of each other in those days, mustn't they?'

'I'm sure of it,' said Lottie. 'And then they must have quarrelled. And parted. And they bisected us in just the same way as they bisected Mummy's christian name.'

'They really ought to have asked us before they cut us in half.'

32

'But at that time we hadn't even learnt to speak.'

The two sisters smiled helplessly. Then they linked arms and went into the garden.

*

The post had come. Everywhere, in the grass, on the wall, and on the garden benches, little girls were sitting, reading letters.

The post had come

Lottie held in her hands the photograph of a man of about thirty-five. She was looking with loving eyes at her father. So that was how he looked. And this was the sort of feeling you had round your heart when you had a real, live father!

Lisa read what he had written to her: 'My dearest, only child!' – 'What a liar!' she said, looking up. 'He knows perfectly well he has twins!' She went on reading: 'I think you must have quite forgotten what your old father looks like. Otherwise you wouldn't be so anxious to have a photograph of him just before the end of the holidays. First I thought I would send you a picture of me as a baby – one that shows me lying naked on a polar-bear skin. But you wrote that it must be an absolutely brand new one. So I rushed off to the photographer's, though I really couldn't spare the time, and explained to him just why I needed it in such a hurry.... I told him that unless he took my picture my Lisa wouldn't recognize me when I went to the station to meet her. By good luck he saw how important it was. And so you're getting it in good time. I'm sorry for the young lady supervisors at your holiday home. I hope you don't lead them such a dance as you do your father – who sends you a thousand greetings and is longing to have you home again.'

'Lovely!' said Lottie. 'And funny! And yet on the picture he looks quite serious.'

'He was probably too shy to laugh in front of the photographer,' speculated Lisa. 'He always looks serious in front of other people. But when we're alone he can be quite jolly.'

Lottie held the photograph tight. 'Can I really keep it?'

'Of course,' said Lisa. 'That's why I got him to send it.'

*

Chubby-faced Steffie was sitting on a bench with a letter in her hands, crying. She wasn't making a sound.

34

The tears streamed down her round, immobile, childish face.

Trudie sauntered by, stopped curiously, went and sat down by Steffie, and looked at her expectantly.

Christine came up and sat down on the other side of Steffie.

Lisa and Lottie approached and stopped. 'Is anything wrong?' asked Lisa.

Steffie continued to cry silently. Suddenly she looked down and said in a flat voice, 'My Mummy and Daddy are going to be divorced.'

'What a mean thing!' cried Trudie. 'They send you off on your holidays, and then do a thing like that. Behind your back!'

'I think Daddy loves another woman,' sobbed Steffie.

Lisa and Lottie walked quickly away. What they had just heard had stirred them to the depths.

'*Our* father,' said Lottie, 'hasn't got a new wife, has he?'

'No,' returned Lisa. 'I should have known if he had.'

'Perhaps one he's not married to?' asked Lottie hesitantly.

Lisa shook her curly head. 'Of course he's got friends. Women friends too. But he doesn't know them all that well. I say, what about Mummy? Has Mummy a – a man friend?'

'No,' said Lottie confidently. 'Mummy has me and her work, and that's all she asks of life, she says.'

Lisa gave her sister a puzzled look. 'Yes, but why are they divorced?'

Lottie thought for a while. 'I wonder if they ever went to Court. I mean, like Steffie's parents want to do.'

'Why is Daddy in Vienna and Mummy in Munich?' asked Lisa. 'Why did they cut us in half?'

'Why', went on Lottie broodingly, 'did they never tell us that we were not just separate, that we were really twins? And why has Daddy never told you that Mummy's still living?'

'Mummy's never told you that Daddy's still living either.' Lisa put her hands on her hips and stuck out her elbows. 'Fine parents we've got, haven't we? Just wait till we tell them a few home truths. That'll make them sit up!'

'We couldn't do that,' said Lottie timidly. 'We're only children.'

'*Only!*' exclaimed Lisa, and threw back her head.

Chapter 4

THE holidays were coming to an end. The piles of clean clothes had melted in the lockers. Regret for what they were leaving kept pace with joy at the prospect of returning home.

Mrs Mutesius was planning a garden-party. The father of one of the girls was the proprietor of a big store, and he had sent a packing-case full of Chinese lanterns, coloured paper-garlands, and such like. Now helpers and children were hard at work decorating the veranda and the garden. They lugged pairs of steps from tree to tree, hung the gaudy lanterns among the foliage, slung garlands from bough to bough, and fixed up a lucky dip on a long table. Others were writing numbers on slips of paper. The first prize was a pair of roller skates with ball-bearings.

'Where have Curls and Plaits got to?' asked Miss Ulrica. (Such were her new names for Lisa and Lottie.)

'Oh *them*!' said Monica contemptuously. 'They'll be sitting in the grass somewhere, holding hands so that the wind won't blow them apart.'

*

The twins were not sitting in the grass somewhere, but in the café garden at the forester's. Nor were they holding hands – they had no time for such things.

Lottie was dictating to the industriously scribbling Lisa

Each had in front of her an octavo notebook, and in her hand a lead pencil, and at that moment Lottie was dictating to the industriously scribbling Lisa: 'Mummy's favourite dish is beef-stew with noodles. You get the beef at Huber's. Half a pound of prime spare-rib.'

Lisa looked up. 'Huber, family butcher, corner of Max Emanuel Street and Prince Eugene Street,' she recited.

Lottie nodded approvingly. 'The cookery book is in the kitchen cupboard on the left of the bottom shelf, and it's got in it all the recipes I know.'

Lisa wrote down: 'Cookery book ... kitchen cupboard ... left of bottom shelf ...' Then she propped her elbows on the table. 'I'm scared stiff of cooking,' she said. 'But if anything goes wrong in the first few days I could say I've forgotten how to do it in the holidays.'

Lottie nodded doubtfully. 'After all, you can write me at once if things go wrong. I shall go to the post office every day and ask if there's a letter for me.'

'So shall I,' said Lisa. 'Mind you write often, and have some jolly good meals at the Imperial. Daddy's always so pleased when I eat a lot.'

'What a pity stuffed pancakes are your favourite dish,' complained Lottie. 'Well, it can't be helped. But I'd rather have had veal cutlet or goulash.'

'If you eat three pancakes the first day, or four or five, you can say you have had enough to last you the rest of your life,' suggested Lisa.

'Yes, I might do that,' answered her sister. But the

very thought of five pancakes made her stomach turn over. She wasn't going to let that worry her, however.

Then the two girls bent over their notebooks again, and heard each other say the names of class-mates, their positions in class, the habits of teachers, and the quickest way to school.

'It's easier for you to go to school than me,' said Lisa. 'All you have to do is to tell Trudie to call for you the first morning. She does call for me sometimes. And then you just let her show you the way, while you carefully notice the street corners and all the rest of it.'

Lottie nodded. Then she gave a start. 'I say, there's something I forgot to tell you – Don't forget to give Mummy a good-night kiss when she puts you to bed!'

Lisa looked blankly in front of her. 'I needn't write that down. I'm not likely to forget *that*!'

*

Can you see what was hatching? The twins had decided not to tell their parents that they knew the truth. They did not want to confront their father and mother with the need to make decisions. They felt they had no right to do so.

And they were afraid that the decisions their parents would make might destroy their happiness now and for the future. But still less could they bring themselves to take the other course – to go back to the homes they had left as though nothing had happened, go on living in the half-world assigned to them unasked by their parents. No! In short, a conspiracy was afoot, and the fantastic plan they had made, born of unsatisfied yearnings and the spirit of adventure, was this: they would swop clothes, hair-styles, trunks, pinafores, and private lives! Lisa would 'go home' with tidy plaits (and determined to be tidy in other ways too), just as though she were Lottie, go home to the mother she knew only from a photograph. And Lottie would go to her father in Vienna with long curls and the will to be as merry and bright as she knew how.

They made most careful preparations for their future adventures. The octavo notebooks were crammed full of notes. They agreed to write to each other *poste restante* in case of a crisis, or if anything important or unexpected should happen.

Perhaps by keeping a sharp look-out they would succeed in the end in unravelling the mystery of why their parents were living apart. And perhaps one fine, one wonderful day, they would live with each other and with *both* parents – but they scarcely dared think, much less speak, of anything so wonderful and remote.

They decided to make the garden-party, on the eve of their departure, a dress rehearsal. Lottie appeared as the curly-headed, high-spirited Lisa. Lisa appeared with plaits as the demure Lottie. And both played their parts to perfection. No one had a clue! Not even Trudie, Lisa's school-friend from Vienna. Each found it thrilling to call out to the other by her own name. Lottie was so full of beans that she turned somersaults, and Lisa behaved with such gentleness and

41

modesty that you would have thought she couldn't say boo to the butter, and a goose wouldn't melt in her mouth.

The Chinese lanterns gleamed among the summer leaves. The garlands swayed in the evening breeze. The party and the holidays were coming to an end. The prizes were being distributed round the lucky dip. Steffie, poor little thing, had drawn the first prize. The roller skates with ball-bearings. (Better small comfort than none at all!)

At last, still playing their parts, the two girls were asleep in each other's beds, dreaming strange, excited dreams. Lottie, for instance, was met at the station in Vienna by a more than life-sized photograph of her father, and standing beside him was a cook in a tall white hat, with a trolly full of steaming stuffed pancakes – ugh!

*

Next morning, at the crack of dawn, two trains, coming from opposite directions, steamed into the station at Egern, near Bohrlaken, on Lake Bohren. Dozens of little girls climbed chattering into the compartments.

Lottie leaned out of the window. From a window of the other train Lisa waved to her. They smiled to give each other courage. Their hearts were thumping, their nerves growing tauter and tauter. If the engines had not begun to hiss and spit at that moment, who knows? – Perhaps those two little girls might still have –

But no! The time-table decided otherwise. The

42

guards waved their flags. The trains began to move simultaneously. The children waved their hands.

Lottie was going as Lisa to Vienna.
Lisa was going as Lottie to Munich.

Chapter 5

THE main station at Munich. Platform 16. The engine came to a halt and gasped for breath. Islands of reunion have formed in the sea of travellers. Little girls were hugging their beaming parents. Happy and excited with the flood of news, people forgot they were in the station and acted as though they were already at home.

But gradually the platform emptied.

And at last there was only one little girl left, a girl with plaits tied in ribbons. She had had curls up to yesterday. Up to yesterday her name had been Lisa Palfy.

At last she squatted down on her trunk and set her teeth grimly. To wait at the station in a strange town, to wait for your mother whom you have never seen except in a photograph and who isn't there to meet you – that's not funny!

Mrs Lisalotte Palfy, *née* Horn, who had resumed the name of Lisalotte Horn after her divorce six and a half years ago, had been held up at the office of the *Munich Illustrated*, where she worked as picture-editor. Some new photographs had just come in for the news pages.

At last she managed to grab a taxi. At last she won the battle for a platform ticket. At last, and at the double, she arrived at platform 16.

The platform was empty?

No! Right at the far end was a child sitting on a trunk. The young woman flashed down the platform like a fire-engine.

The knees of the little girl squatting on the trunk were trembling. An unsuspected feeling welled up in her childish heart. That real, radiant, living, flashing young woman was her mother!

'Mummy!' Lisa ran towards her, held out her arms, and threw them round her neck.

'My little housekeeper!' whispered the young woman with tears in her eyes. 'At last, at last, I've got you back!'

The little girl's mouth kissed the soft cheeks passionately, the gentle eyes, the lips, the hair, the cute little hat. Yes, even the hat!

*

Up in the restaurant and down in the kitchen of the Hotel Imperial there was benevolent excitement. A little girl, favourite of all regular customers and of the staff, daughter of Mr Palfy, conductor at the Opera House, had come home again!

45

Lottie – I beg your pardon! – Lisa was in her usual place, her hereditary chair with the two big cushions, eating stuffed pancakes as though her life depended on it.

The regular customers came over to the table, one by one, stroked the little girl's curly hair, patted her gently on the shoulder, asked how she had enjoyed herself, remarked that after all no place could be nicer than Vienna with Daddy there, placed all kinds of presents on the table – toffees, chocolates, pralines, coloured pencils, yes, one even took from his pocket a little old-fashioned needle-case and observed a little awkwardly that it had been the property of his late grandmother. Then they nodded to Mr Palfy, the conductor, and went back to their tables. Today they were really going to enjoy their lunch again, poor lonely uncles!

But no one had a better appetite than Mr Palfy himself. He had always strongly emphasized the need of 'all true artists' to be alone; he had always thought his late marriage a mistake, a step into the humdrum, middle-class world; but today he experienced a warm, family feeling that was most 'inartistic'. And when his daughter took his hand with a shy smile, as though to prevent his running away, then, although he wasn't eating Irish stew, he felt something like a dumpling in his throat.

Hello, here's Franz the waiter again, waddling up with another pancake.

Lottie shook her curls. 'I couldn't possibly, Mr Franz!'

46

'But, Lisa!' cried the waiter reproachfully. 'It's only the fifth!'

When the mildly disquieted Franz had waddled back to the kitchen with the fifth pancake, Lottie plucked up her courage. 'Do you know, Daddy,' she said, 'in future I'm always going to have the same food as you.'

'You don't say?' cried Mr Palfy. 'But how about when I eat smoked ham? You know you can't stand smoked ham. It makes you feel sick.'

'When you eat smoked ham,' she said miserably, 'I'll have pancakes again.' (After all it is not quite so easy being your own sister!) And then?

And then Dr Strobel appeared with Peterkin. Peterkin was a dog. 'Look, Peterkin,' said the doctor with a smile. 'See who's here! Go and say how-d'ye-do to Lisa.'

Peterkin wagged his tail and trotted quickly up to the Palfy's table to say how-d'ye-do to his old friend, Lisa.

Here's a fine how-d'ye-do! When Peterkin arrived at the table he sniffed at the little girl, turned round, and trotted straight back to his master.

'What a stupid dog,' remarked Dr Strobel ill-humouredly. 'Can't even recognize his best friend! Just because she's been away in the country for a week or two. And people talk a lot of windy nonsense about the unfailing instinct of animals!'

But Lottie thought to herself, 'What a good thing that doctors are not as clever as dogs!'

*

Dr Strobel appeared with Peterkin

Mr Palfy, accompanied by his daughter, the trunk, the presents, a doll, and a bag containing Lottie's bathing things, had arrived at his flat in Rotenturm Street. And Rosa, Mr Palfy's housekeeper, had been beside herself with joy at seeing the child again.

But Lottie knew from what Lisa had told her that Rosa was a two-faced cat, and was merely putting on an act. Daddy, of course, did not notice it. Men never notice anything.

He fished a ticket out of his wallet and gave it to his daughter. 'This evening I'm conducting Humperdinck's *Hänsel and Gretel*,' he said. 'Rosa will bring you to the Opera House and fetch you home at the end of the performance.'

'Oh!' Lottie beamed. 'Can I see you from where I'm sitting?'

'Certainly you can.'

'And will you look at me sometimes?'

'Of course.'

'And may I give a little wave when you look at me?'

'Yes, and I'll wave back to you, Lisa.'

Then the telephone rang. A feminine voice was speaking from the other end. Lottie's father replied to her mainly in monosyllables. But when he had put down the receiver he seemed to be in rather a hurry. He had to be alone for a few hours. Yes, a composition! For, you see, he was not only a conductor, he was also a composer. And he simply *could* not compose at home. No, he did his composing in a studio in Ring Street, which he had taken expressly for the purpose. So –

'I'll see you at lunch tomorrow in the Imperial.'

'And I may wave to you in the opera, Daddy?'

'Of course, my dear. Why not?'

A kiss on the grave, childish brow. Then his hat on the knobbly artist's head.

The door slammed.

The little girl walked slowly to the window and thought with some uneasiness about life. They wouldn't let her mother work at home; and her father *couldn't* work at home. What a handful parents are!

But since she was a determined and practical little girl – largely on account of her mother's training – she soon dropped these gloomy reflections, armed herself with the octavo notebook, and began, with the help of Lisa's instructions, a voyage of discovery, room by room, through that fine flat in old Vienna.

When she had completed her investigations, she sat down by sheer force of habit, took up the house-keeping-book that lay there on the kitchen table, and worked one by one through the columns of figures.

In doing so she noticed two things: first, that Rosa, the housekeeper, had made a mistake on practically every page, and, second, that every one of these mistakes was to Rosa's advantage.

'Now then! What's this mean?' Rosa was standing at the kitchen door.

'I've been adding up the figures in your book,' said Lottie in a low but firm voice.

'Fine goings on!' cried Rosa indignantly. 'You do your sums in school. That's the place for sums.'

'I shall always add up your books,' declared Lottie gently, and hopped off the kitchen chair. 'We learn *in*

Rosa was standing at the kitchen door

school, but not *for* school, that's what my teacher says.' And with that she stalked out of the room.

Rosa looked after her, flabbergasted.

❊

Dear readers, old and young, male and female! I have regretfully come to the conclusion that it is about

A film star, famous all over the world

time I told you something of Lisa's and Lottie's parents, and especially of how they came to be living apart.

If, at this point, a grown-up person peeps over your shoulder and exclaims, 'Oh, *him*! How, in heaven's name, can he write such things for *children*!' then please read the grown-up person the following:

'When Shirley Temple was no more than seven or eight she was already a film star, famous all over the world. And she earned for the film companies many millions of dollars. But when Shirley wished to go with her mother to a cinema and take a look at a Shirley Temple film, she was not admitted. She was still too young. It was forbidden. She could only *make* films. That was *not* forbidden. She was old enough for that.'

If the grown-up person who peeps over your shoulder does not understand this example of Shirley Temple and its connexion with Lisa's and Lottie's parents and their divorce, then give him my very kind regards, and tell him from me that there are large numbers of divorced parents in the world and large numbers of children who suffer in consequence. And there are also large numbers of other children who suffer because their parents are *not* divorced. But since children have to suffer from such things, it is far too nice-minded, indeed it is positively wrong, *not* to tell children about them in an understanding and understandable way.

Very well then! Arnold Palfy, the orchestral conductor, was an artist, and artists are well known to be strange creatures. He did not wear, it is true, a broad-brimmed hat or a flapping tie. On the contrary, he was very nicely dressed – neat, almost smart.

But his inner life! That was complex! Oh, his inner life, that was another story altogether! When he had an idea for a composition he found it absolutely essential to go away immediately and be alone, so that he could note it down and develop it. Such an idea might come when he was at a big party. 'What's become of Palfy?' asks his host. And somebody answers, 'He's probably had an idea!' Then the host smiles sourly, but thinks to himself, 'What manners! A man can't run away, whenever he gets an idea!' But Mr Palfy could, and did!

He even used to run out of his own flat when he was just married, young, in love, ambitious, happy, and crazy, all at the same time.

And then, when the little twins howled day and night in the flat, and the Vienna Philharmonic Orchestra was about to give the first performance of his first piano concerto, he had his grand piano carted away and installed in a studio in Ring Street, a studio he had taken in a state of artistic desperation.

At that time he had a great-many ideas, and so it happened that he seldom came home to his young wife and the howling twins.

Lisalotte Palfy, *née* Horn, barely twenty years of age, did not find it very cheerful. And when it reached her barely-twenty-year-old ears that her husband was not only composing music in his studio, but also studying vocal parts with sopranos and contraltos who thought him very sweet, she got desperate and applied for a divorce.

So now Conductor Palfy, who had been so concerned for his creative peace, was well out of it. Now he could be alone as much as he liked. He engaged a capable nurse in Rotenturm Street to look after the one twin that remained to him after the divorce. And, as he had so earnestly desired, not a soul bothered him.

And suddenly that did not suit him either. Oh, these artists! They really don't know what they want. All the same he went on industriously composing and conducting, and grew more famous year by year. Besides, when a fit of blues took him, he could go to his flat in Rotenturm Street and play with his baby daughter, Lisa.

Whenever there was a concert in Munich at which a new work by Arnold Palfy was being played, Lisalotte Horn bought herself a ticket, and sat with bowed head in one of the cheap seats at the back, and thus learned from her ex-husband's music that he had not grown any happier. In spite of his success. And in spite of being alone.

Chapter 6

MRS LISALOTTE HORN just had time to take her daughter home to her tiny flat in Max Emanuel Street and rush back, at full speed and very unwillingly, to her office. Work was waiting for her, and work does not like waiting.

Lisa – I beg your pardon! – Lottie took a first careful look round the flat. Then she collected the keys, her mother's purse, and a net bag and set out to do the shopping.

At Huber's, the butcher's, at the corner of Prince Eugene Street, she bought half a pound of beef, prime spare-rib, and some kidneys and a few bones. Now she was desperately searching for Mrs Wagental's, the greengrocer's, where she wished to buy mixed herbs, noodles, and salt.

At Huber's, the butcher's

Annie Habersetzer was not a little surprised to catch sight of her school-fellow, Lottie Horn, standing in the middle of the road, attentively turning the pages of an octavo notebook.

'Do you do your homework in the street?' she asked curiously. 'Don't you know we're still on holiday?'

Lisa stared at her in bewilderment. It is maddening to be accosted by someone you are supposed to know well when you have never seen them before in your life! At last she pulled herself together and said brightly, 'Hullo! Why not come along? I've got to go to Mrs Wagental's for some mixed herbs.' Then she put her arm through that of the strange girl – if only she knew that freckled youngster's christian name! – and let her unconsciously pilot her to Mrs Wagental's shop.

Mrs Wagental was naturally glad to see Lottie Horn back from her holidays, and with such red cheeks, too! When Lisa had bought what she wanted, Mrs Wagental gave each of the girls a toffee and asked them to remember her kindly to Mrs Horn and Mrs Habersetzer.

That took a load off Lisa's mind. At last she knew that the other girl was Annie Habersetzer. (This is what the octavo notebook said about her: 'Annie Habersetzer – I've had a row with her three times. She bullies the smaller girls, especially Elsa Merck, who is the smallest girl in the class.') Well, that was enough to start with.

When they parted outside her house, Lisa said to her, 'And that reminds me, Annie. We've fallen out

Mrs Wagental was glad to see her

three times already about Elsa Merck and all that. You know what I mean. Next time I shan't just talk to you, I shall –' And with that she made an unmistakable movement of her hand and ran off.

'We'll see about that,' thought Annie furiously. 'We'll see about it in the morning. She must have gone crackers during the holidays.'

*

Lisa was cooking. She had put on one of Mummy's aprons, and was spinning to and fro like a top between the gas-cooker, where the saucepans were boiling over the gas-jets, and the table on which lay the open cookery-book. Every few minutes she lifted a saucepan-lid. When the boiling water hissed and boiled over, she jumped. How much salt should she put in the noodles? 'Half a teaspoonful!' How much celery salt? 'A pinch!' How much, for goodness' sake, is a pinch? And then, 'Grate a nutmeg.' Where were the nutmegs? Where was the grater?

She rummaged in drawers, climbed on chairs, looked into all the canisters, glanced at the clock on the wall. She jumped down from a chair, grabbed a fork, lifted a lid, burned her fingers, squealed, stabbed the beef with the fork – No, it wasn't done yet.

She stood stock still, holding the fork in her hand. What was she looking for? Oh yes, the nutmeg and grater. Goodness! What was that lying so harmlessly beside the cookery-book? – The mixed herbs. They had to be cleaned and put in the broth! Down with the fork, up with the knife. Was the meat done yet?

And where were the gratemeg and the nutter? Oh dear, the grater and the nutmeg? The mixed herbs had first to be washed under the tap, and the carrots had to be scraped. Ah-uh! You had to watch out that you didn't cut yourself! And when the meat was done you had to take it out of the saucepan and drain off the bones. For that you needed a colander. And Mummy would be here in half an hour! And twenty minutes before she arrived you had to drop the noodles in boiling water. What a mess the kitchen was in! And the nutmeg! And the colander! And the grater! And... and ... and ...

Lisa flopped down on a kitchen chair. Oh Lottie! It's not so easy being your own sister! Hotel Imperial ... Dr Strobel ... Peterkin ... Franz ... And Daddy ... Daddy ... Daddy ...

The clock ticked on.

In twenty-nine minutes Mummy would be here! ... In twenty-eight and a half minutes! ... In twenty-eight minutes! ... In twenty-seven and a half minutes!

Lisa clenched her fists with determination and got up to start again. As she did so, she growled to herself. 'If I can't manage this –'

But that's the queer thing about cooking. Determination is all very well if you want to jump off a tower. But will-power is not enough when it comes to cooking beef and noodles.

And when Mrs Horn came home, tired with the day's exertions, she did not find a smiling little housekeeper awaiting her. Not at all. She found a completely exhausted scrap of misery, a slightly damaged, confused, crumpled little object, from whose mouth, twisted ready for tears, came the words, 'Mummy, don't be angry! I think I've unlearnt cooking.'

'But, Lottie, you can't unlearn cooking,' cried her mother, surprised. But there was not much time for surprise. There were childish tears to dry. Broth to taste, overcooked meat to add to it, plates and knives and forks to be fetched from the dresser, and many other things to do.

When at last they were sitting under the lamp in the living-room, eating the noodle-soup, Mrs Horn said comfortingly, 'It tastes all right in spite of everything, doesn't it?'

'Does it?' A timid smile stole across her daughter's face. 'Does it, really?'

Her mother nodded and smiled back reassuringly.

Lisa breathed again. And now suddenly the food really tasted better than anything she had ever eaten in her life. Notwithstanding the Hotel Imperial and the stuffed pancakes.

'I'll do the cooking myself for a day or two,' said her mother. 'You can watch me. Then you'll soon be as good as you were before the holidays.'

Lisa nodded vigorously. 'Perhaps even better,' she said, with a touch of sauciness.

After the meal they washed up together, and Lisa told her mother what a grand time she had had at the holiday home. (But she did not breathe a word about the other girl who was the living image of herself.)

*

Meanwhile Lottie was sitting, dressed in Lisa's prettiest frock, pressed close to the plush front of a dress-

How well the musicians obeyed him

circle box at the Vienna Opera House, looking down with shining eyes at the orchestra, where Mr Palfy was conducting the overture to *Hänsel and Gretel*.

How wonderful Daddy looked in evening clothes. And how well the musicians obeyed him, although there were some quite old gentlemen among them. When he made masterful, threatening movements with his baton they played as loud as a thunderstorm. And when he wanted them to play softly, they made noises like an evening breeze. How frightened they must be of him! And yet a few minutes ago when he waved up at the box, he had looked so jolly.

The door of the box opened.

A fashionable young lady swept in, sat down near the front, and smiled at Lottie as the child looked up.

Lottie turned away shyly and went on watching her Daddy conducting the orchestra.

The young lady produced a pair of opera-glasses. And a box of chocolates. And a programme. And a powder-compact. She went on producing things until the plush front of the box was like a shop-window.

At the end of the overture the audience loudly applauded. Conductor Palfy bowed repeatedly. And then, as he lifted his baton again, he looked up at the box.

Lottie waved her hand shyly. This time Daddy smiled even more sweetly than before.

And then Lottie noticed that she was not the only one waving. The lady at her side was waving too.

Was she waving to Daddy? Was it possible that Daddy had smiled so sweetly at the young lady? And not at his little daughter? And why had Lisa never told her about this strange woman? Had Daddy met her only recently? If so, how came she to be waving to him so intimately? Lottie made a mental note: 'Write to Lisa tonight. Ask if she knows anything? Post it tomorrow on the way to school. Address – *Poste restante*, Forget-me-not, Munich 18.'

Then the curtain rose, and the fate of Hänsel and Gretel called for all her sympathy. Lottie held her breath. Down on the stage the parents were sending their children into the forest to get rid of them. And yet they were fond of them! How could they be so wicked? Or were they? Was it only *what they were doing* that was wicked? It only made them unhappy, so why did they do it?

Lottie, the bisected and substituted twin, grew more and more agitated. Though she was not fully aware of it, her emotional conflict was concerned less and less with the two children and their parents down there on the stage, and more and more with herself, her twin sister, and her own parents. Had they the right to do what they had done? Mummy was not in the least wicked; neither was Daddy. Yet what they had *done*, that *was* wicked. The woodman and his wife were so poor that they could not buy food for their children. But Daddy? Had Daddy ever been poor?

Later, when Hänsel and Gretel arrived outside the gingerbread-house, picked pieces off the walls, and were startled by the voice of the witch, Miss Irene Gerlach – for that was the fashionable lady's name – leant over to Lottie, pushed the box of chocolates

65

towards her, and whispered, 'Would you like something to nibble, too?'

Lottie jumped, looked up, saw the woman's face close to hers, and threw out her hand in self-defence. But her hand caught the box of sweets and swept it off the front of the box and, as if in response to a cue, there was a shower of chocolates in the stalls! Heads turned and looked up. Suppressed laughter mingled with the music. Miss Gerlach smiled, half-embarrassed, half-annoyed.

Lottie went stiff with fright. She was wrenched suddenly out of the dangerous magic of art. She found herself suddenly in the dangerous world of reality.

'I beg your pardon,' she murmured.

The lady smiled forgiveness. 'It doesn't matter, Lisa,' she said.

Perhaps she was a witch. A more beautiful witch than the one on the stage.

*

Lisa was lying in bed in Munich for the first time. Her mother was sitting on the edge of the bed. 'There, Lottie dear,' she said. 'Sleep well! And pleasant dreams!'

'If I'm not too tired,' muttered Lisa. 'You won't be long, will you?'

There was a larger bed by the opposite wall. On the turned-back coverlet was Mummy's nightdress ready to slip into.

'I'm coming,' said her mother. 'As soon as you're asleep.'

Lisa threw her arms round her mother's neck and

gave her a kiss. Then another and another. 'Good night!'

The young woman hugged her little daughter. 'I'm so happy to have you back,' she said softly. 'You're all I've got now!'

Lisa's head sank back sleepily. Lisalotte Palfy, *née* Horn, tucked in the bedclothes and listened for a while to her daughter's breathing. Then she rose quietly and tip-toed back into the living-room.

Her brief-case lay there under the standard lamp. She still had a lot of work to do.

*

Lottie had been put to bed for the first time by sulky Rosa. Soon afterwards she stealthily got up again and wrote the letter she intended to drop in the post-box early next morning. Then she got quietly back into Lisa's bed and, before switching off the light, examined the nursery again at her leisure.

It was a spacious, attractive room with a frieze of fairy-tale figures round the walls, a cupboard for toys, a bookshelf, a desk for doing homework, a big toy shop, a graceful, old-fashioned dressing-table, a doll's perambulator, and a doll's bed. Nothing was missing except the one thing that mattered.

Had she not sometimes – quite secretly, so that Mummy would not suspect – wished for just such a beautiful room as this? And now that she had it, a sharp pain, pointed with envy and longing, bored into her heart. She longed for the modest little bedroom where her sister was now lying, for Mummy's good-night kiss, for the beam of light under the door of the living-room; for the sound of that door quietly opening, of Mummy stopping beside her bed, stepping over on tiptoe to her own bed, slipping into her nightie, and snuggling down between the sheets.

If only Daddy's bed were there, or at least in the next room! Perhaps he would snore. That would be heavenly. Then she would know that he was near. But he was not near: he was sleeping in another flat – in Ring Street. Perhaps he wasn't even sleeping. Perhaps he was sitting with the fashionable chocolate-lady, in a great, glittering room, drinking wine, laughing, dancing with her, nodding affectionately to her – as he had done at the opera – to *her*, not to his little daughter, who had waved so happily and timidly from the box.

Lottie fell asleep. She had a dream. The story of the poor father and mother, who sent Hänsel and Gretel into the forest because they had no food for them, became entangled with her own fears and unhappiness.

Lottie and Lisa are sitting – in the dream – on the same bed, staring with terrified eyes at a door through which many bakers enter, in white caps, carrying loaves of bread. They pile up the loaves against the walls. More and more bakers come and go. The piles of loaves grow higher. The room gets smaller and smaller.

Then her father is standing there in his evening clothes, with lively movements conducting the parade of bakers. Mummy comes rushing in and asks anxiously, 'But, Arnold, what's to happen now?'

'We must send the children away!' he shouts

Lottie had a dream

angrily. 'There's no more room for them. There are too many loaves in the house!'

Mummy wrings her hands. The children sob wretchedly.

'Get out!' he cries and raises his conductor's baton threateningly. Then the bed rolls obediently to the window. The casements spring open. The bed floats out of the window.

It flies over a big city, across a river, over hills, fields, mountains, and forests. Then it dips back to earth again and lands in a great thicket of trees, like a primitive forest, which reverberates frighteningly with the uncanny croaking of birds and the roaring of wild beasts. The two little girls sit up in bed, paralysed with fear.

There is a rustling and crackling in the thicket. The children throw themselves down and pull the bedclothes over their heads. And now the witch comes out of the undergrowth. But she is not the witch that was on the stage of the Opera House; she looks much more like the chocolate-lady in the box. She surveys the bed through her opera-glasses, nods her head, smiles very haughtily, and claps her hands three times.

As though at a word of command, the dark wood is transformed into a sunny meadow. And in the meadow is a house, built of chocolate-boxes, with a fence consisting of bars of chocolate. Birds twitter gaily, marzipan hares hop about in the grass, and all around are shining golden nests full of Easter eggs. A little bird alights on the bed and sings such pretty trills that Lottie and Lisa emerge from the bedclothes,

though at first only as far as the tips of their noses
When they see the meadow with the marzipan hares,
the chocolate-eggs, and the chocolate-house, they
jump quickly out of bed and run to the fence. There
they stand in amazement in their long nightgowns.
'Special mixture!' reads Lisa aloud. 'And croquettes!
And nougat-centres!'

'And bitter selection!' cries Lottie delightedly.
(For even in her dreams she does not care for sickly
sweets.)

Lisa breaks a large piece of chocolate from the
fence. 'Nut-milk!' she says greedily and raises it to
her lips.

At that the witch's laughter echoes from the house.
The children start. Lisa throws the chocolate away.

And there comes Mummy panting across the
meadow with a large wheelbarrow full of loaves.

'Stop, children!' she cries in horror. It's all
poisoned!'

'We were so hungry, Mummy!'

'Here are loaves of bread for you. I couldn't get
away from the office any earlier.' She throws her
arms round them and tries to drag them away.
But suddenly the door of the chocolate-house
opens. Daddy appears with a big saw such as wood-
cutters use, and shouts, 'Leave the children alone,
Mrs Horn!'

'They are *my* children, Mr Palfy!'

'Mine *too*,' he shouts back. And, as he comes towards them, he explains dryly, 'I'll cut the children
in half. With the saw! I get half of Lottie and half of
Lisa, and you get the same, Mrs Horn!'

71

The trembling twins have jumped back into bed.

Mummy spreads out her arms and stands protectingly in front of the bed. 'Never, Mr Palfy!'

But Daddy pushes her aside and begins, starting at the head of the bed, to saw through it. The saw shrieks to freeze your blood, and moves inch by inch down the length of the bed.

'Let go of each other's hands,' Daddy orders.

The saw comes nearer and nearer to the intertwined hands of the two sisters, nearer and still nearer. It is on the point of slicing the flesh.

Mummy cries broken-heartedly.

They can hear the witch chuckling.

Then the children's hands release each other.

The saw cuts down between them till the bed is sawn completely in two and becomes two beds, each with four legs.

'Which twin will you have, Mrs Horn?'

'Both! Both!'

'Sorry,' says the man. 'Fair's fair. Well, if you can't make up your mind, I'll have this one. I don't care which. I can't tell them apart anyhow.' He seizes one of the beds. 'Which are you then?'

'Lisa!' she cries. 'But you can't do it!'

'No!' screams Lottie. 'You can't bisect us!'

'Hold your tongue,' says the man sternly. 'Parents can do as they like.' With that, he walks towards the chocolate-house, dragging the one bed behind him on a string. The chocolate-fence opens of its own accord.

Lisa and Lottie wave to each other despairingly.

'We'll write!' shouts Lisa.

'*Poste restante!*' shouts Lottie. 'Forget-me-not, Munich 18!'

Daddy and Lisa disappear into the house. Then the house itself vanishes, as though it has been wiped out.

Mummy throws her arms round Lottie. 'Now we two are all forlorn,' she says sadly. Suddenly she stares doubtfully at Lottie. 'Which of my daughters are you? You look like Lottie.'

'I *am* Lottie!'

'No, you look like Lisa ...'

'I *am* Lisa!'

Mummy looks into her daughter's eyes with a startled expression, and says – speaking somehow in Daddy's voice – 'Now curls, now plaits! The same heads, the same noses!'

And now Lottie has a plait on the left side of her head and curls like Lisa on the right. The tears stream down her cheeks. And she says wretchedly, 'Now I don't know which I am. Oh, poor half, poor me!'

Chapter 7

WEEKS have gone by since the twins' first day and first night among strangers in a strange world. Weeks when every minute, every casual incident, every encounter, threatened danger and discovery. Weeks with a good deal of palpitation and many *poste restante* letters demanding urgent and additional information.

But everything turned out for the best. Partly, of course, by good luck. Lisa had 'again' become an expert cook. The teachers in Munich had got more or less used to the fact that the little Horn girl had come back from her holidays less industrious, less tidy and attentive, but, on the other hand. more lively and quick in the uptake.

And the teachers in Vienna were quite pleased to find that Conductor Palfy's daughter worked harder in class and was much better at arithmetic. Only yesterday in the teachers' room, Miss Gestettner had remarked, rather pompously, to Miss Bruckbaur: 'It is a most instructive experience, my dear Miss Bruckbaur, for anyone interested in pedagogics, to follow the development of Lisa Palfy – to see an excess of temperament changing into quiet, controlled, and effective strength; high spirits, fun, and a fitful desire for knowledge into a constant and conscientious effort towards education. Well, my dear Miss Bruckbaur, one might almost call it unique. And don't forget that this transformation, this metamorphosis of a character into something higher and more disciplined, has arisen from the child's inner resources, without any educative pressure from without.'

Miss Bruckbaur nodded momentously and answered: 'This unfolding of character, this individual will to achieve form, is apparent also in the changes in Lisa's handwriting. I always say that handwriting and character –' But, thank goodness, we don't need to listen to what Miss Bruckbaur always said.

Let us rather give unstinting recognition to Peterkin, Dr Strobel's dog, which for some time had resumed its old habit of saying how-d'ye-do to the little girl at Conductor Palfy's table. It had resigned itself to the fact, although it was beyond its canine comprehension, that Lisa no longer smelt like Lisa. Human beings are capable of *so* many things – Why not of that too? Besides, she did not eat so many stuffed pancakes as before and seemed to have developed a healthy appetite for meat. When you consider that there are no bones in pancakes, while you can be fairly certain of finding them in chops, you can easily understand how Dr Strobel's dog had overcome its initial reserve.

If Lisa's teachers found a surprising change in Lisa – what would they have thought, supposing they had known her, of Rosa, the housekeeper? For Rosa – of that there can be no doubt – had become quite a different person. Perhaps she was not essentially deceitful and idle and slatternly. Perhaps she was like that only because no one had kept a sharp eye on her.

Since Lottie had been there, gently but inexorably

checking up and finding out all there was to be known about the household, Rosa had developed into a model housekeeper.

Lottie had persuaded her father to hand over the housekeeping money to her instead of giving it to Rosa. And it was quite comic to see Rosa knock at the nursery-door, go in, and ask a nine-year-old girl, who was sitting gravely at her desk doing her homework, for some housekeeping money. Rosa reported faithfully what she wanted to buy, what she would dish up for supper, and the other necessary household details.

Lottie would quickly tot up the cost, take the money out of her desk, hand it over to Rosa, write down the amount in an exercise book, and then, in the evening, there was a general settling-up over the kitchen table.

Even her father had noticed that less money was spent on the housekeeping, that, though the household cost him less, there were always fresh flowers on the table – even in his studio in Ring Street – and that altogether things were much more homely in Rotenturm Street. ('Just as if there were a woman in the house,' he thought to himself, and the idea startled him quite a bit.)

Miss Irene Gerlach, the chocolate-lady, had noticed that Mr Palfy spent more and more time at his flat. And, in a way, she had challenged him about it. Very circumspectly, of course, for artists are sensitive people.

'Do you know,' he said to her, 'when I came in the other day, Lisa was sitting at the piano strumming away happily at the keys. And she was singing a little song, too. Quite sweet! And yet in the old days she wouldn't have gone near a piano if you had tried to drag her there with a tractor.'

'And?' asked Miss Gerlach. And her eyebrows went up till they nearly reached the line of her hair.

'And?' Mr Palfy gave an embarrassed laugh. 'Since then I've been giving her piano-lessons. She finds it great fun. So do I.'

Miss Gerlach looked quite contemptuous. For she was an intellectual. Then she said pointedly, 'I thought you were a composer, not a piano-teacher for little girls.'

No one would have dared in the old days to say that to Mr Palfy to his face. But he laughed like a schoolboy. 'But I've never composed so much in my life as I'm doing now,' he cried, 'or such good stuff!'

'What is it going to be?' she asked.

'A children's opera,' he answered.

*

So her teachers thought Lisa had changed, Lottie thought Rosa and Peterkin had changed, and her father thought the flat in Rotenturm Street had changed. What a lot of changes!

And in Munich there had been all kinds of changes too. When her mother noticed that Lottie was no longer so domesticated at home or so hard-working at school, but seemed to have become more mercurial and high-spirited, she went into committee with herself and this is the kind of thing she said:

'Now, Lisalotte, you had a tractable little child and, instead of letting her *be* a child, you made her into a housekeeper. Then she spent a few short weeks with children of her own age by a lake in the mountains and became what she ought to have been all along – a happy little girl, whom your troubles hardly worry at all. You've been much too egoistic. Shame on you! You ought to be delighted that Lottie is happy and care-free. What if she does smash a plate when washing up? What if she does bring home a letter from her teacher saying that in recent weeks she has become much less attentive, tidy, and industrious, and that, only yesterday, she gave her school-fellow, Annie Habersetzer, on four separate occasions, a good hard smack? However many troubles a mother has to bear, her first duty is to guard her child, lest it be driven too soon out of the paradise of childhood.'

Thus Mrs Horn spoke seriously to herself, and much more of the same kind. And at last, one day, she spoke to Miss Linnekogel, her daughter's formmistress. 'I want my child,' she said, 'to be a child and not a stunted little grown-up! I would rather she was a happy, genuine little girl than have her forced at all costs to be your best pupil.'

'But Lottie used to manage to combine both qualities,' returned Miss Linnekogel, slightly piqued.

'Why she cannot do so any longer, I do not know. As a woman who has to earn her own living, I don't know enough in many ways about my daughter. The change must be connected in some way with the summer holidays. But I know one thing – she can no longer be what she used to be. And that is all that matters.'

Miss Linnekogel grasped energetically at her spectacles: 'I, as your daughter's teacher and guide, must have other aims in view for her. I must and shall attempt to restore your child's inner harmony.'

'Do you really think that a bit of inattention in the arithmetic lesson and a few blots in her exercise book –'

Miss Linnekogel grasped at her spectacles

'A good example, Mrs Horn! Her exercise book! Lottie's writing shows clearly how much she has lost her – how shall I put it? – her spiritual balance. But let us leave the question of her writing. Do you think it right that Lottie should take to hitting the other girls?'

'Girls!' Mrs Horn intentionally emphasized the plural. 'As far as I know she has hit no one but Annie Habersetzer.'

'Isn't that enough?'

'And this Annie Habersetzer thoroughly deserved it. She had it coming to her.'

'But, Mrs Horn!'

'A big greedy girl who vents her spite on the smallest child in the class – I should not expect her teacher to defend her.'

'I beg your pardon? Really? I had no idea.'

'Then ask poor little Elsa Merck. Perhaps she can tell you something about it.'

'But why didn't Lottie tell me when I punished her?'

Then Mrs Horn threw out her chest a little and answered, 'Perhaps she hadn't – how did you put it? – enough spiritual balance.' Then she dashed off to the office. She had to take a taxi to get there in time. Two marks and thirty pfennigs. Oh dear, what a lot of money!

*

Suddenly at noon on Saturday, Mummy packed a rucksack. 'Put on your strong shoes,' she said. 'We're going to Garmisch, and we shan't be back till to-morrow night.'

Her daughter asked, rather anxiously, 'Mummy, can we afford it?'

Mrs Horn felt a kind of little stab. Then she laughed. 'If we spend all our money, I shall have to sell you.'

Her daughter danced with glee. 'Fine! And when you've got the money, I shall give my purchasers the slip. And when you've sold me three or four times,

80

we shall have so much that you won't need to work for a month.'

'Are you worth as much as all that?'

'Three thousand marks and eleven pfennigs! And I shall take my mouth-organ.'

What a week-end it was! Like raspberries and whipped cream! From Garmisch they tramped through the forest, passing a lovely lake, and on to Lake Eib. Playing the mouth-organ and singing songs. Then down through tall woods, slipping and stumbling. They found wild strawberries. And lovely, mysterious flowers, lily-like Turk's cap and many-blossomed, lilac-coloured gentian, and mosses with little, spiked helmets on their heads. And tiny alpine violets that smelt sweet beyond belief. That evening they reached a village. There they took a room with one bed. And when they had eaten an immense supper from their rucksack, they left the guest-room, and slept together in the one bed! Outside in the fields the grasshoppers sang a thin serenade. On Sunday morning they went on their way.

A great, snow-capped mountain shone white as silver. Men and women in peasant-costume were coming out of church. Cows stood around in the village street as though gossiping over their elevenses.

And then on again. That was a tough bit of walking. My hat! Near some grazing horses, amidst millions of meadow-flowers, they ate boiled eggs and cheese sandwiches, and followed them up with a short afternoon nap in the grass. Later they dropped down, between wild raspberry-canes and dancing butterflies, back to Lake Eib. Cowbells tinkled to ring

Lake Eib

In the afternoon. They saw, crawling along the sky, the cable-railway to the snow-capped peak. The lake looked tiny in the bowl of the valley.

'As though God had thrown down a two-mark piece,' said Lisa thoughtfully.

Of course they bathed in Lake Eib. And Mummy stood coffee and cakes on the hotel-terrace. And then it was high time to take the road back to Garmisch.

Tanned and happy they sat in the train. And the nice gentleman opposite obstinately refused to believe that the girl sitting next to Lisa was really her mother and had to earn her own living.

At home they dropped into their beds like sacks of potatoes. The last thing Lisa said was, 'Mummy, today was lovely! Lovelier than anything in the world!'

Her mother lay awake for a while. How often in the past she had deprived her daughter of pleasures that might easily have been hers. Well, it was not too late. She could still make up for it.

Then Mrs Horn fell asleep also. A smile dreamed on her face and flitted across her cheeks like the wind over Lake Eib.

Her daughter had changed. And now the young mother was beginning to change too.

Chapter 8

LOTTIE's talent for the piano was lying fallow. It was not her fault. But of late her father had not had much time for giving lessons. Perhaps that was because of his work on the children's opera? May be. Or was it? Well, little girls have a way of knowing when something is wrong. When fathers talk of children's operas and never speak of fashionable young ladies, their daughters know which way the wind is blowing.

*

Lottie came out of the Rotenturm-Street flat and rang the bell of the flat next door. A painter named Gabel lived there, a nice, friendly man, who had said he would like to make a drawing of Lottie when she could spare the time. Mr Gabel opened the door. 'Oh, it's Lisa!'

'I've got time today,' she said.

'Just a minute,' he answered. He slipped into his studio, took a big rug from the sofa and hung it over a painting that stood on his easel. He was just painting an antique scene from the classics. Such scenes are not always suitable for small children.

Then he invited Lottie in, placed her in an armchair, took up a block, and began to sketch. 'You don't play the piano these days,' he remarked.

'Did it disturb you very much?'

'Not a bit. On the contrary, I've missed it.'

84

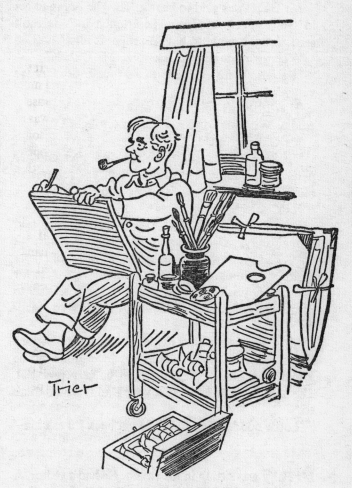

Mr Gabel took up a block and began to sketch

'Daddy hasn't much time now,' she said solemnly. 'He's composing an opera. A children's opera.'

Mr Gabel was glad to hear it. Then he began to get irritable. 'These windows,' he grumbled. 'You can't see a thing. I ought to have a proper studio.'

'Then why don't you take one, Mr Gabel?'

'Because there are none to be found. Studios are very scarce.'

The little girl said, after a pause, 'Daddy has a studio. With big windows. And a top-light.'

Mr Gabel grunted.

'In Ring Street,' added Lottie. And after another pause, 'You don't need so much light for composing music as you do for painting, do you?'

'No,' said Mr Gabel.

Lottie groped her way a step further. She said thoughtfully, 'Daddy could even change flats with you. Then you would have bigger windows and more light for painting. And Daddy would have a place for composing just next to our flat!' The idea seemed to please her immensely. 'Wouldn't that be very practical?'

Mr Gabel could have made all kinds of objections to Lottie's idea. But it would not have done. So he said with a smile, 'Yes, it would be very practical. The only question is whether your Daddy would think so.'

Lottie nodded. 'As soon as I get back I'll ask him.'

*

Mr Palfy was sitting in his studio. He had a visitor. A lady visitor. Miss Irene Gerlach had 'happened' to have some shopping to do in the neighbourhood, and so she had thought to herself, 'I'll just drop in and see Arnold. Why not?'

So Arnold had put aside the pages of the score on which he had been working, and was chatting with Irene. At first he was a little angry, for he could not for the life of him stand people dropping in and interrupting his work without first making an appointment. But gradually he yielded to the pleasure of sitting with this charming lady and stroking her hand almost by accident.

Irene Gerlach knew what she wanted. She wanted to marry Mr Palfy. He was famous. She liked him. He liked her. So there were no insuperable difficulties in the way. It is true that he knew nothing as yet of his future happiness. But she would tactfully let him know in good time. And he would end up by imagining that the idea of marriage had come to him quite spontaneously.

But there was *one* obstacle – that stupid child! Though when Irene had presented Arnold with a baby or two that would all come right of itself. Irene Gerlach would find a way to handle that shy, serious little girl!

The bell rang.

Arnold opened the door.

And who stood in the doorway? The shy serious little girl. She had a bunch of flowers in her hand, and she curseyed and said, 'Hullo, Daddy, I've brought you some fresh flowers.' Then she walked into the studio, curtseyed slightly to the visitor, picked up a vase, and disappeared into the kitchen.

Irene smiled maliciously. 'When I see you with your daughter I have the impression that she keeps you under her thumb.'

The composer laughed awkwardly. 'She's been acting lately in a very determined way, and what she does is entirely right – so what can I do?'

As Miss Gerlach shrugged her pretty shoulders Lottie appeared on the scene again. First she put the fresh flowers on the table. Then she brought out cups and saucers and said to her father, as she distributed them around the table, 'I'll make some coffee. We must offer your visitor some refreshment.'

Daddy and his visitor looked after her with some perplexity. 'And I thought the child was shy!' Miss Gerlach reflected. 'Heavens, what a fool I was!'

In a few minutes Lottie reappeared with coffee, sugar, and cream. She poured out the coffee – quite the housewife! – asked if Miss Gerlach took sugar, handed her the cream, sat down beside her father. Then she said with a friendly smile, 'I'll just have a cup to keep you company.'

Mr Palfy poured her out a cup of coffee and asked politely, 'How much cream, madam?'

Lottie giggled. 'Half and half, if you please, sir.'

'There you are, madam.'

'Thank you very much, sir.'

They drank the coffee. They sat in silence. At last Lottie opened the conversation. 'I've just been to see Mr Gabel.'

'Has he been drawing you?' asked her father.

'Only a bit,' she said. Another sip of coffee, then she added innocently, 'He hasn't enough light. What he needs most of all is a top-light. Like you've got here....'

'Then he should take a studio with a top-light,' remarked the conductor, very trenchantly but without a suspicion that he was moving in the precise direction where his daughter wanted him.

'I told him that,' she explained calmly. 'But all the studios are let.'

'The little beast!' thought Miss Gerlach, who, being also a daughter of Eve, saw just what the child was aiming at. Here it came:

'You don't really need a top-light for composing, Daddy, do you?'

'No, not really.'

Lottie took a deep breath, looked hard at the front of her dress and said, as though the question had just occurred to her, 'Suppose you were to swop with Mr Gabel, Daddy?' Thank heaven, she had got it out at last! Lottie squinted up sideways at her father. Her eyes were full of timid entreaty.

Half irritable, half amused, he glanced from the little girl to the fashionable lady, who had just time to conjure up a gently ironic smile.

'Then Mr Gabel would have his studio,' said the child, and her voice shook a little, 'with all the light he needs. And you would work just next to the flat. Next to Rosa and me.' Lottie's eyes went down on their knees, if one may so express it, before her father's. 'You would be just as much alone as you are here. And when you don't want to be alone you can come across the landing and be with us. You won't even need to put your hat on. And we can have lunch at home. When the lunch is ready, we'll give three rings at your bell. We'll always have your favourite dishes – even smoked ham. And when you play the piano we shall be able to hear it through the wall ...' The childish voice had grown more and more uncertain. Now it stopped.

Miss Gerlach suddenly rose from her chair. She had to hurry home. How the time had passed! But the conversation had been just too terribly interesting!

Mr Palfy saw his visitor out. He kissed her scented ladylike hand. 'Till tonight,' he said.

'Perhaps you will be otherwise engaged?'

'How do you mean, darling?'

She smiled. 'Perhaps you will be moving house.'

He laughed.

'Don't laugh too soon! From what I know of your daughter, she has already made arrangements with the furniture removers.' The lady swept off furiously down the stairs.

When Mr Palfy came back into the studio, Lottie was already washing up the coffee cups. He played a few notes on the piano. He walked up and down with long strides. He stared at the notes he had scribbled on the score.

Lottie took care not to make a noise with the cups and saucers. When she had wiped them dry and put them back in the cupboard, she put on her hat and went quietly into the studio.

'Good-bye, Daddy ...'

'Good-bye.'

'Are you coming home to supper?'

'No. Not today.'

The little girl nodded slowly and timidly held out her hand.

'Listen, Lisa, I don't like other people interfering in my affairs, not even my own daughter! I know myself what's good for me.'

'Of course, Daddy,' she said calmly and gently. She was still holding out her hand.

At last he took it and, as he did so, he saw that there were tears on her eyelashes.

A father must know when to be firm. So he pretended not to notice anything unusual, nodded shortly, and sat down at his grand piano.

Lottie went softly to the door, softly opened it, and was gone.

Mr Palfy ran his fingers through his hair. Childish tears! Another distraction to cope with! And he was trying to compose a children's opera! It was enough to drive one to drink! He could hardly endure seeing a little thing like that with tears in her eyes. They hung on her long lashes like dewdrops on tiny blades of grass.

His hands struck a few notes. He bent his head and listened. He played the phrase again. He repeated it in another key. It was the minor variation of a jolly song he had written for his opera. He altered the rhythm. And he went on working.

What use are childish tears? An artist can get away with murder. He just takes his music paper and writes down a few notes. And presently he will lean back and rub his hands complacently because he has just composed a sweet, touching song in C minor.

(Isn't there a giant about somewhere who will put the man across his knee occasionally?)

*

More weeks have passed. Miss Irene Gerlach had not forgotten the little scene in the studio. And as for Lottie's proposal that her father should exchange his flat in Ring Street for Mr Gabel's, Miss Gerlach had understood it for what it was: a challenge to battle! Essentially a woman – and Irene Gerlach was essentially a woman, despite the fact that Lottie could not stand her – she was quick to accept the challenge. She knew her weapons. She knew how to use them. She knew how effective they were. She had shot all her arrows into that quivering target, the artistic heart of Mr Palfy. Every shot had been a bull's-eye. Every barbed shaft was stuck firmly in the heart of her beloved enemy. He was quite helpless.

'I want you to be my wife,' he said, and it sounded like a savage command.

She stroked his hair, smiled, and said with a little mockery, 'Tomorrow I'll put on my best frock, darling, and go and ask your daughter's consent.'

Another arrow was sticking in his heart. And this time it was a poisoned one.

*

Mr Gabel was sketching Lottie. Suddenly he lowered his block and pencil and said, 'What's wrong with you today, Lisa? You look like a wet week-end!'

The little girl took a long breath, as though she had a heap of stones on her chest. 'Oh, it's nothing much.'

92

'Anything to do with school?'

She shook her head. 'That wouldn't worry me.'

Mr Gabel laid down his block. 'Do you know what we'll do, you little misery? We'll pack up for today.' He stood up. 'Let's go for a walk. That will help to take your mind off it.'

'I think I'll play the piano a bit.'

'Better still,' he said. 'I shall hear you through the wall. So I shall get something out of it too.'

She shook his hand, curtseyed, and went out.

He looked thoughtfully after her. He knew how heavy trouble can weigh on a child's heart. He had been a child himself once and, unlike a good many people, had not forgotten it.

When the strum of a piano came from the neighbouring flat, he nodded approvingly and began to whistle the tune. Then he jerked the covering from the easel, took up his brush and palette, studied his work with screwed-up eyes, and got on with the job.

*

Mr Arnold Palfy arrived home at his flat in Rotenturm Street. The stairs seemed twice as high as usual. He hung his hat and coat on a hook in the cloakroom. So Lisa was playing the piano? Well, she would have to stop and listen to him for a bit. He straightened his jacket as though he were about to pay a call on the director of the opera. Then he opened the door of the sitting-room.

The little girl looked up from the keys and smiled to him. 'Daddy? How lovely!' She jumped down

from the piano-stool. 'Shall I make you some coffee?'
She turned to go to the kitchen.

He caught her arm. 'No, thank you,' he said. 'I
want to talk to you. Sit down!'

She sat down in a big, winged armchair, where she
looked no bigger than a doll, smoothed out her check
skirt, and looked up at him expectantly.

He cleared his throat nervously, took a few steps
up and down, and finally stopped in front of her.
'Well, Lisa,' he began, 'I want to talk to you about
a serious and important matter. I have been alone
since your mother – er – since your mother has not
been here. That's seven years. Of course not entirely
alone, for I've had you. And I have you still.'

The child looked up at him, wide-eyed.

'What rot I'm talking,' he thought. He was rather
annoyed with himself. 'In short,' he went on, 'I don't
wish to be alone any longer. There's going to be a
change. In my life and therefore in yours too.'

The room was very still.

A fly buzzed loudly as it tried to butt its way
through the window-pane into the fresh air outside.
(Anyone could have told it that it was a pure waste of
time and could only result in damage to its insect
head. Flies are just stupid, but people – people are
clever, aren't they?)

'I have decided to marry again.'

'No!' said the little girl clearly. It sounded like a
cry. Then she repeated softly, 'No, please, Daddy!
No, please! Please, please, no!'

'You know Miss Gerlach. She's very fond of you.
And she'll make you a good mother. It would not be

right for you to go on growing up in a household that lacks all feminine influence.' (Wasn't he touching? There was only one thing more he could have said – that he was marrying simply to give his child a mother!)

Lottie went on shaking her head and moving her lips without saying anything. Like an automaton that cannot stop working. It looked frightening.

So her father glanced quickly away again, and said, 'You will get used to the new situation more quickly than you think. Cruel stepmothers only happen in fairy tales. So I know I can rely on you, Lisa. You are the most sensible little person I've ever come across.' He looked at the clock. 'There! Now I must go. I've got to rehearse *Rigoletto* with Mr Luser.'

He was gone. The little girl sat there stupefied.

Mr Palfy reached the cloakroom and replaced his hat on his artistic head. Then there was a cry from the room. 'Daddy!' It sounded as though someone were drowning.

'People don't drown in sitting-rooms,' thought Mr Palfy, and slipped out. He was in a great hurry. For of course he had to rehearse with Mr Luser.

*

Lottie had awakened from her stupor. Even in her despair her common sense did not desert her. What was she to do? For unquestionably she had to do something. Daddy could never marry another woman, never! He already had a wife. Even if she was not living with him. Never would Lottie accept a new mother, never! She *had* a mother, her Mummy

95

whom she loved more than anyone else in the world!

Perhaps Mummy could help. But Lottie could not let her know. She could not let her into the two children's big secret, and least of all could she tell her that her father wanted to marry this Miss Gerlach.

So there was only one way left, and Lottie had to go that way herself.

She got the telephone directory. She turned the pages with trembling fingers. 'Gerlach.' There were not very many Gerlachs. 'Gerlach, Stefan. Managing-director, Vienna Hotel Company, 43, Kollmann Avenue.'

Daddy had mentioned recently that Miss Gerlach's father owned a number of restaurants and hotels, including the Imperial, where they went every day to luncheon. '43, Kollmann Avenue!'

When Rosa had explained how to get to Kollman Avenue, Lottie put on her hat and coat. 'I'm going out now,' she said.

'What are you going to Kollmann Avenue for?' asked Rosa curiously.

'I want to speak to someone.'

'Well, don't be long.'

Lottie nodded and set out.

*

A parlourmaid entered Irene Gerlach's charming room and smiled. 'There's a child to see you, madam. A little girl.'

Madam had just revarnished her finger-nails and was waving her hands in the air to help dry the varnish. 'A little girl?'

'Her name is Lisa Palfy.'

'Ah,' said Madam, with a slight drawl. 'Show her in!'

The parlourmaid withdrew. The young lady rose, threw a glance at herself in the mirror, and could not suppress a smile at her tense and earnest expression.

As Lottie entered the room Miss Gerlach said to the parlourmaid, 'Make us some chocolate, and bring some éclairs.' Then she turned graciously to her visitor. 'How sweet of you to come and see me. It shows how thoughtless I am. I ought to have invited you long ago. Won't you take your coat off?'

'No, thank you,' said Lottie. 'I won't stay long.'

'Oh?' Irene Gerlach lost nothing of her patronizing manner. 'But you'll have time to sit down?' Lottie perched herself on the edge of a chair, never taking her eyes off the lady.

Irene Gerlach began to find the situation awkward and ridiculous. But she controlled herself. After all, there was something at stake. Something she was anxious to win, something she was determined to win. 'I suppose you just happened to be passing this way?'

'No. I have something to say to you.'

Irene Gerlach smiled enchantingly. 'I am all ears. What is it?'

Lottie got off the chair, stood in the middle of the room, and said slowly, 'Daddy said you wanted to marry him.'

'Did he really say that?' Miss Gerlach's laugh was clear as a bell. 'Didn't he really say that he wished to marry me? Still, that doesn't really matter. It's quite true, Lisa. Your father and I wish to marry. And you and I are going to get on well together. I'm quite sure of it. Aren't you? Listen, when we have lived together for a little while we shall be the best of friends. We'll both do all we can, won't we?'

Lottie stepped back and said emphatically, 'You mustn't marry Daddy.'

This was certainly going too far. 'And why not?'

'Because you mustn't.'

'Not a very good reason,' said the young lady sharply. Kindness was getting her nowhere. 'Are you trying to forbid me to marry your father?'

'Yes!'

'Well, I've never heard such nonsense!' She was becoming agitated. 'I must ask you to go home now. I don't know whether I shall tell your father of this curious visit. I'll think it over. But if I don't tell him, it will be because I don't want to put serious obstacles in the way of our future friendship. For I still want to believe that we shall be friends. *Auf Wiedersehen!*'

Lottie turned again at the door, and said: 'Leave us alone! Please, please ...' Then she was gone.

Miss Gerlach decided there was only one thing to do – hasten the preparations for the marriage. And when that was over, she must arrange to send the child away to a boarding-school. Nothing would help but strict discipline at the hands of strangers.

'What do *you* want?'

The parlourmaid was there with the tray. 'I've brought the chocolate. And the éclairs. What's become of the little girl?'

'Get out!'

*

98

Mr Palfy did not come home to dinner for he was conducting at the Opera House. Rosa kept Lottie company, as she always did in her father's absence.

'You're not eating a thing,' remarked Rosa reproachfully. 'And you look like a ghost. I feel quite frightened. What's the matter?'

Lottie shook her head and said nothing. The housekeeper took Lottie's hand and quickly dropped it again. 'You're feverish! Off to bed with you!' Then, panting and groaning, she carried the completely apathetic child into the nursery, undressed her, and put her to bed.

'Don't tell Daddy!' muttered Lottie. Her teeth were chattering. Rosa piled up blankets and pillows. Then she ran to the telephone and called up Dr Strobel.

The old gentleman promised to come at once. He was as worried as Rosa.

She telephoned to the Opera House. 'All right,' someone answered. 'We'll tell Mr Palfy at the interval.'

Rosa flew back to the bedroom. Lottie was tossing about in the bed, stammering confused, meaningless words. The pillows and blankets were on the floor.

If only Dr Strobel would come! What should she do? Compresses? But what sort? Hot? Cold? Wet? Dry?

*

Conductor Palfy, in a white tie and tails, was spending the interval in the soprano's dressing-room. They drank a little wine together and talked shop. Theatre people have only one topic of conversation – the theatre. That cannot be helped. There was a knock at the door.

The stage manager entered. 'We've had a call from your home in Rotenturm Street. Your daughter has been suddenly taken ill. Dr Strobel was called immediately and by this time he ought to be at her bedside.' The conductor turned very pale.

'Thank you, Herman,' he said in a low voice. The stage manager withdrew.

'I hope it's nothing serious,' said the soprano. 'Has she had measles?'

'No,' he said, and got up. 'Excuse me, Mitzi!' As the door closed behind him, he broke into a run.

He was telephoning. 'Hullo, Irene!'

'Yes, darling? Is the performance over so soon? I'm not nearly ready to come out.'

He told her hurriedly what he had just heard. Then he said, 'I'm afraid I shan't be able to take you out tonight.'

'Of course not. I hope it's nothing serious. Has she had measles?'

'No,' he answered impatiently. 'I'll ring you again in the morning.' Then he put down the receiver.

A gong sounded. The interval was over. Life and the opera went on.

*

At last the opera was over. The conductor was racing up the stairs in Rotenturm Street. Rosa let him in. She still had her hat on, for she had just been out to the chemist's.

Dr Strobel was sitting at the bedside.

'How is she?' asked her father in a whisper.

'Not at all well,' answered the doctor. 'But you needn't whisper. I've given her an injection.'

Lottie lay on the pillows, flushed and fighting for breath. Her face was drawn as though the artificial sleep which the old doctor had imposed on her distressed her.

'Measles?'

'Not a trace.'

Rosa entered the room, snuffling back her tears.

'For goodness' sake take your hat off!' cried the conductor irritably.

'Oh, dear! Excuse me!' She removed her hat and held it in her hand.

Dr Strobel looked inquiringly from one to the other.

'She is evidently going through a severe nervous crisis,' he said. 'Do you know what could have caused it? No? Well, have you a suspicion?'

Rosa said, 'I don't know whether this has anything to do with it, but – she went out this afternoon. She said she had to speak to someone. And before she went she asked me the way to Kollmann Avenue.'

'Kollmann Avenue?' repeated the doctor, and looked at Mr Palfy.

Mr Palfy went quickly into the next room and telephoned. 'Did Lisa come to see you this afternoon?'

'Yes,' said a feminine voice. 'But how came she to tell you?'

He made no reply to that, but asked further, 'What did she want?'

Miss Gerlach laughed shortly. 'You had better ask her yourself.'

'Answer, please!' It was lucky she could not see his face.

'If you want to know, she came to forbid me to marry you,' she returned sharply.

He mumbled something and put down the receiver. 'What's the matter with her?' asked Miss Gerlach. Then she became aware that she had been cut off. 'The little beast!' she exclaimed, half-aloud. 'She sticks at nothing! Goes off to bed and pretends to be ill!'

*

The doctor gave a few further instructions and prepared to leave. Mr Palfy detained him at the door. 'What's wrong with the child?'

'A nervous fever. I'll look in first thing tomorrow morning. Good night.'

The conductor went into the nursery, sat down by the bed, and said to Rosa, 'I shan't need you any more. Good night.'

'But hadn't I better –'

He looked at her.

She went. She still had her hat in her hand.

He stroked the little, hot cheek. Lottie started in her feverish sleep and writhed away from him.

He looked round the room. Her school-satchel lay ready packed on the seat by the desk. And beside it lay Christel, her doll.

He got up stealthily, fetched Christel, put out the light, and sat down by the bed again.

He sat in the dark, stroking the doll as though it were a child. A child that did not start away from the touch of his hand.

Chapter 9

MR BERNAU, editor of the *Munich Illustrated*, groaned aloud. 'The silly season, my dear! Where can we get a front-page news-picture without thieving?'

Mrs Horn, standing beside his writing-desk, remarked, 'Neo-Press has sent some photos of the new women's breast-stroke champion.'

'Is she pretty?'

The young woman smiled: 'Passable for a swimmer.'

Mr Bernau waved the idea aside with an air of dejection. Then he began to ransack his desk.

'Some comic village photographer sent me in some pictures the other day. Photos of twins.' He searched among folders and copies of old newspapers. 'Two enchanting little girls! Alike as two peas! Come on, what's become of you, you little minxes? That sort of thing always goes big. All it needs is a snappy caption. In the absence of news photos, what's wrong with a pair of bonny twins? Ah, here you are!' He had found the envelope. He studied the photographs and nodded approvingly. 'We'll use this, Mrs Horn.' He handed her the photographs.

Presently he looked up, for his picture-editor had not said a word. 'Hullo!' he cried. 'Why you look like Lot's wife, a pillar of salt. Wake up! Do you feel ill, Mrs Horn?'

'Not too well, Mr Bernau.' Her voice shook. 'I'm better now.' She stared at the photograph. She read the name of the sender -- 'Joseph Appeldauer, Photographer, Bohrlaken on Lake Bohren.'

Everything was going round and round in her head.

'Pick out the best picture and write me a caption that'll make our readers' hearts sing for joy. It's just your cup of tea.'

'I wonder if we ought to publish them,' she heard herself say.

'Why not?'

'I don't believe they are genuine.'

'Bit of faking, eh?' Mr Bernau laughed. 'You overrate the good Mr Appeldauer. He's not as clever as all that. Well, to work, my dear! You can leave the caption till the morning, if you like. Let me see it before it goes into print.' He nodded and bent over the next item.

She groped her way back to her room, dropped into her chair, put down the photographs in front of her, and pressed her hands to her brow.

Her thoughts rode roundabouts in her head. The

twins! Bohrlaken! The holidays! Of course! But why had Lottie never said anything about it? Why had not Lottie brought the photographs back with her? For when the twins had their photographs taken they must have meant to bring them home! Then, of course, they found out that they were sisters. And decided to say nothing about it. It was understandable; yes indeed it was. Heavens, how alike they were! Not even the proverbial mother's eye could tell the difference! Oh, my darlings! My two darlings!

If Mr Bernau had put his head round the door at that moment, he would have seen a face overwhelmed with joy and pain; tears streaming down, tears that tire the heart, as though life itself were pouring from one's eyes.

Luckily Mr Bernau did not put his head round the door.

Mrs Horn did her best to pull herself together. This was just the moment to keep one's head. What was to happen? What did she want to happen? She decided to speak to Lottie.

An ice-cold thought went through her. A thought that shook her like an invisible hand.

The girl she would speak to – *was* she Lottie?

*

Mrs Horn had sought out her daughter's teacher, Miss Linnekogel, at her lodgings.

'The question you have asked me,' said Miss Linnekogel, 'is an exceedingly strange one. Do I think it possible that your daughter is not your daughter but another girl? Excuse me, but –'

106

'No, I'm not mad,' Mrs Horn assured her, and laid a photograph on the table.

Miss Linnekogel looked at it. Then at her visitor. Then at the photograph again.

'I have two daughters,' said Mrs Horn in a low voice. 'The second one lives with my divorced husband in Vienna. This photograph happened to come into my hands a few hours ago. I did not know that the two children had met in the holidays.'

Miss Linnekogel opened and closed her mouth like a fish. She shook her head and pushed the photograph away as though she were afraid it would bite her. At last she asked, 'Didn't they know of each other's existence before this meeting?'

Mrs Horn shook her head. 'No. My husband and I agreed when we parted that they should be kept in ignorance. We thought it the best way.'

'And you, yourself, never heard again from your husband or your other daughter?'

'Never.'

'Do you think he has remarried?'

'I don't know. I doubt it. He thought he was unsuited to family life.'

'A most astonishing story,' said the teacher 'Could the children really have hit on the absurd idea of changing places? Even considering the change in Lottie's character – and her writing, Mrs Horn, her writing! – it seems hardly believable, and yet it would certainly provide an explanation for several things.'

Mrs Horn nodded and looked straight in front of her.

'Forgive my frankness,' went on Miss Linnekogel.

'I have never married; I have no children; I am a teacher – but I always think that women, I mean married women, attach too much importance to their husbands. Nothing is really important except the happiness of the children.'

Mrs Horn smiled wryly. 'Do you believe that my children would have been happier if my husband and I had gone on living together unhappily?'

Miss Linnekogel said thoughtfully, 'I'm not reproaching you. You are still very young. You were hardly more than a child when you married. All your life you will be younger than I have ever been. What is right for one may be wrong for another.'

Her visitor stood up.

'And what will you do?'

'If only I knew!' said Mrs Horn.

*

Lisa was standing at the counter of a Munich post office. 'No,' said the clerk in charge of *poste-restante* letters, and his voice was sympathetic, 'No, Miss Forget-me-not, nothing for you again.'

Lisa looked at him doubtfully. 'What can it mean?' she observed miserably.

The clerk tried a little joke. 'Perhaps the not has fallen off the forget-me-not.'

'No fear of that!' she said, as though to herself. 'I'll come again tomorrow.'

'We'll do our best for you,' he said, smiling.

*

When Mrs Horn reached home her heart was a battle-

'No, Miss Forget-me-not, nothing for you'

ground of hot curiosity and cold fear: she could hardly get her breath.

Her daughter was busy in the kitchen. There was a clatter of saucepan lids. Something was simmering in a casserole.

'It smells nice,' said Mrs Horn. 'What's for dinner?'

'Pork chops with spinach and sauté potatoes,' returned her daughter proudly.

'How quickly you've learned to cook!' said Mrs Horn with seeming innocence.

'Yes, haven't I?' answered her daughter gaily, 'I never thought I –' She broke off in alarm and bit her lip. At all costs she must avoid meeting her mother's eye.

Mrs Horn leaned against the doorpost. She was white, white as the wall behind her.

The little girl was at the open cupboard-door, taking out the plates, which clattered together as though there were an earthquake.

Her mother opened her mouth with an effort. 'Lisa!' she said.

Crash!

The plates were in splinters on the floor. Lisa had spun round. Her eyes were wide with fright.

'Lisa!' repeated her mother gently, and held out her arms.

The little girl hung on her mother's neck as though she were drowning. She sobbed passionately.

Her mother fell on her knees and stroked the child with trembling hands. 'My child, my darling child!'

They knelt there among the smashed plates. The pork chops were burning on the stove. There was a smell of charred meat. Water spat and hissed from the saucepans and dripped on the gas-jets.

The woman and the little girl were unaware of all that. They were – as is often said, though seldom truthfully – 'in another world'.

*

Some hours had passed. Lisa had confessed and Mummy had forgiven her. It had been a long, complicated confession, followed by a brief, unspoken absolution for all the sins committed – a look, a kiss. Nothing more was needed.

Now they were sitting on the settee. Lisa had snuggled close, very close, to her mother. Oh, how wonderful it was to have told the truth at last! How free she felt, as free as air! She had to cling tightly to her mother lest she should suddenly float away.

'What an artful pair you are!'

Lisa giggled with pride. (There was *one* secret she had not yet revealed – the existence in Vienna of a certain Miss Gerlach, of whom Lottie had written her several anxious letters.) Her mother sighed.

Lisa looked up apprehensively.

'Well, my dear,' said her mother, 'I'm wondering what's to come next? Can we go on acting as though nothing has happened?'

Lisa shook her head firmly. 'Lottie must be simply longing for you. And you for her, too, Mummy?'

Her mother nodded.

'And I, too,' confessed Lisa, 'for Lottie and –'

'And your father?'

Lisa nodded. Eagerly and yet timidly. 'I only wish I knew why Lottie hasn't written ...'

'Yes,' murmured her mother. 'I'm worried.'

Chapter 10

LOTTIE lay apathetically in bed. She was asleep. She was generally asleep. 'Weakness,' Dr Strobel had said when he called that morning. Mr Palfy was sitting by her bedside, looking down earnestly at her little, thin face. For days he had hardly left the room. They had found another conductor for the Opera House. A camp bed had been brought in from the boxroom.

The telephone rang in the next room. Rosa entered on tiptoe. 'A trunk call from Munich,' she whispered. 'Will you take it?'

He got up quietly, makings signs to her to stay in the room till he returned. Then he stole out to the telephone. Munich? Who could it be? Probably his concert-agents, Keller & Co. Why on earth didn't they leave him in peace?

He took up the receiver and gave his name. The exchange put through the call.

'Palfy speaking.'

'This is Mrs Horn,' said a feminine voice, all the way from Munich.

'What?' he asked in surprise. 'Who? Lisalotte?'

'Yes,' said the distant voice. 'Please forgive me for telephoning. But I'm worried about the child. I hope she's not ill.'

'Yes,' he said softly. 'She is ill.'

'Oh!' The distant voice took on a note of alarm.

Puzzled, Mr Palfy said, 'But I don't understand. How did you –'

'We suspected it. Lisa and I.'

'Lisa?' He laughed nervously. Then he listened with bewilderment. Listened with ever-growing bewilderment. Shook his head. Ran his fingers agitatedly through his hair.

The distant feminine voice hurriedly explained all that could be explained in such breathless haste.

'Are you still speaking?' asked the girl at the switchboard.

'By heavens, yes! Don't cut us off,' shouted Mr Palfy. After all you can more or less imagine the tumult in the poor man's mind.

'What's the matter with the child?' asked the anxious voice of his ex-wife.

'A nervous fever,' he answered. 'She's passed the crisis, the doctor says. But she's worn out, mentally and bodily.'

'A good doctor?'

'Certainly, Dr Strobel. He's known Lisa since she was a baby.' He gave a jangled laugh. 'Sorry! Of course, it's Lottie. No, he hasn't known her.' He sighed.

And away in Munich a woman sighed also. Two grown-up people completely at a loss. Their hearts and tongues paralysed. And their brains too, it seemed.

Into that awkward and dangerous silence broke an eager childish voice. 'Daddy! Daddy dear!' The words echoed across the distance. 'This is Lisa! Hullo, Daddy! Shall we come to Vienna? Shall we come now?'

The saving word had been spoken. The icy constraint of the two grown-ups melted as at the touch of a spring breeze. 'Hello, Lisa!' cried her father, longingly. 'Yes, that's a good idea!'

'You've said it, Daddy!' The little girl laughed joyfully.

'When can you get here?'

Then the young woman's voice came again. 'I'll find out what time the first train leaves in the morning.'

'Take a plane!' he shouted. 'You'll get here quicker.' ... 'How can I shout like that?' he thought. 'I shall wake her up.'

When he got back to the nursery, Rosa surrendered his usual place by the bedside and began to tiptoe towards the door.

'Rosa,' he said softly.

They both stopped.

'My wife's coming tomorrow.'

'Your wife?'

'Ssh! Not so loud! My ex-wife. Lottie's mother.'

'Lottie's?'

He smiled and waved his hand. How was she to know? 'Lisa's coming, too.'

'Lisa? What d'you mean? There's Lisa.' She pointed to the bed.

He shook his head. 'No, that's her twin.'

'Twin?' The poor woman was hopelessly out of her depth in the family relationships of Conductor Palfy.

'See that there's enough to eat. We'll talk about the sleeping arrangements later.'

114

'Well, God bless my soul!' she muttered, as she crept from the room.

Mr Palfy looked at the exhausted and slumbering child. Her brow glistened with moisture. He took a towel and gently dabbed her face and forehead.

So this was his other little daughter! His Lottie! What courage and strength of mind she had shown before sickness and despair overwhelmed her! She could scarcely have got that courage from her father. From whom, then?

From her mother?

The telephone rang again. Rosa put her head round the door. 'Miss Gerlach.'

Mr Palfy shook his head without looking up.

*

Mrs Horn was given leave of absence by Mr Bernau to attend to 'urgent family affairs'.

She telephoned to the airport, and was lucky enough to get two seats on a plane leaving early the following morning. Then she packed the bare necessities into a suitcase.

Short as it was, the night seemed endless. But even endless-seeming nights end sometime.

*

Next morning, as Dr Strobel, accompanied by Peterkin, arrived outside the house in Rotenturm Street, a taxi drove up. A little girl jumped out of the taxi, and Peterkin sprang at her as though he had suddenly gone mad. He barked, spun round like a top, whimpered with joy, and sprang at her again.

'Hullo, Peterkin! Hullo, Doctor!'

The doctor was too astounded to answer. Suddenly he too sprang at the child – though not as gracefully as Peterkin – and shouted. 'Have you gone crazy? Get back to bed at once!'

Lisa and Peterkin made a dash for the house. A young lady alighted from the cab.

'That child will catch her death!' cried the doctor, horrified.

'She's not the child you think,' said the young lady pleasantly. 'She's her sister.'

*

Rosa opened the door of the flat. She found herself facing a yapping dog and a little girl.

'Hullo, Rosa,' said the little girl, and she and Peterkin dashed into the nursery.

The housekeeper looked limply after them, and crossed herself.

Then old Dr Strobel came panting up the stairs. With him came a very pretty young woman carrying a suitcase.

'How's Lottie?' asked the woman quickly.

'A little better, I think,' said Rosa. 'Can I show you in?'

'I know the way, thank you.' And the strange woman also disappeared into the nursery.

'When you've come round a bit,' said the doctor, with a chuckle, 'perhaps you'll help me off with my coat. But take your time.'

Rosa started. 'I beg your pardon, sir,' she stammered.

'I don't need to hurry so much today,' he explained patiently.

'Mummy!' breathed Lottie. Her eyes, big and shining, hung on her mother's face as though it were a phantom of dream and magic. The young woman silently stroked the hot, childish hand. She knelt by the bed and took her trembling little daughter gently in her arms.

Lisa threw a lightning glance at her father, who was standing by the window. Then she found some employment with Lottie's pillows. She beat them, turned them, and smoothed out the sheets. *She* was the little housekeeper now. She had learned it from her mother.

Mr Palfy stole a sideways glance at the three of them, the mother with her children. *His* children, too, of course. And the young mother had been, years ago, his young wife. Submerged days, forgotten hours, rose up before him. A long, long time ago ...

Peterkin lay at the foot of the bed as though struck by lightning and kept looking from one little girl to the other. Even the black-enamelled tip of his little nose twitched doubtfully towards each child in turn, as though he could not decide what to do next. What a shame to put a nice, affectionate dog into such a quandary!

There was a knock at the door.

The four occupants of the room awoke as though from a strange, waking sleep.

The old doctor came in, jovial and rather noisy as usual. He crossed to the bed. 'How's the patient?'

117

'Fi-i-ine!' said Lottie, with a worn smile.

'Any sign of an appetite today?' he growled.

'If Mummy cooks,' whispered Lottie. Mummy nodded and went over to the window. 'Forgive me, Arnold, for not having spoken to you before.'

Mr Palfy shook hands with her. 'I'm grateful to you for coming.'

'Not at all! What else could I do? The child –'

'Of course, the child,' he returned. 'Still, I'm grateful.'

'You look as though you hadn't slept for days,' she said uncertainly.

'I shall make up for it. I was anxious about – about the child.'

'She'll soon be all right again,' said the young woman confidently. 'I feel it.'

A certain amount of whispering was going on at the bed. Lisa bent close to Lottie's ear. 'Mummy doesn't know about Miss Gerlach. We must never tell her either.'

Lottie nodded anxiously.

Old Dr Strobel could not have heard what they said because he was reading the thermometer. Though of course he was not reading it with his ears. And if, after all, he did hear something, no one knew better than he how to avoid showing it.

'The temperature's almost normal,' he announced. 'You're over the worst of it. Congratulations, Lisa.'

'Thank you,' said the real Lisa, giggling.

'Or do you mean me?' asked Lottie, smiling warily, for her head was still aching.

'You're a pair of conspiring females,' he growled. 'A fine couple of intriguing minxes! You've even led my Peterkin up the garden path.'

He put out his two massive hands and gently stroked the girls' heads. Then he gave a powerful cough and got up. 'Come, Peterkin! If you can tear yourself away from these mountebanks.'

Peterkin wagged his tail in farewell. Then he snuggled close against the vast trouser-leg of the doctor, who was just remarking to Mr Palfy, 'A mother's a kind of medicine you can't buy at the chemist's!' He turned to the young woman. 'Can you stay till Lisa – Oh, confound it! – till Lottie is quite well again?'

'I think I can. I should like to.'

'Then that's settled,' said the old gentleman. 'Your ex-husband will just have to make the best of it.'

Mr Palfy opened his mouth.

'Don't bother to say it,' said the doctor, laughing. 'I know what it will do to your artistic temperament having all these people in the flat! Have patience! You'll soon be nice and lonely again.'

He was in form today, the old doctor! He opened the door so suddenly that Rosa, who was listening outside, got a good-sized bump. She put both hands to her buzzing forehead.

'Lay the blade of a cold clean knife on it,' he prescribed, every inch the doctor. 'That's all right. I'll give you that valuable advice for nothing!'

*

Night had spread its wings over the earth. In Vienna as everywhere else. There was no sound in the nursery. Lisa was sleeping. Lottie was sleeping too, sleeping herself back to health.

Up to a few minutes ago Mrs Horn and Mr Palfy had been seated in the next room. They had discussed a great many things and had avoided discussing many more. Mr Palfy got up. 'Well, I must be off,' he said. As he spoke he felt – and rightly – rather a fool. Remember that two little girls of nine were sleeping in the next room, and the pretty young woman standing opposite him was their mother, and yet he had to sneak off like the big boy of the dancing class who has just been snubbed! Sneaking out of his own flat! If there were still such things as invisible familiar spirits – as there used to be in the good old days – how they must have chuckled!

She went with him to the door.

He hesitated. 'If she gets worse, you can get me at the studio.'

'You needn't worry,' she said confidently. 'And don't forget you have a lot of sleep to make up.'

He nodded. 'Good night.'

'Good night.'

As he went slowly down the stairs she called softly, 'Arnold!' He looked back inquiringly.

'Will you be coming back to breakfast?'

'Yes.'

When she had locked and bolted the door she stood for a time thinking. He had aged. No doubt of that. He looked almost like a real grown-up man, her ex-husband.

120

Then she went to keep watch over her sleeping children – hers and his!

*

An hour later a fashionable young lady alighted from a car outside a house in Ring Street and parleyed with a disobliging porter.

'Conductor Palfy?' he grunted. 'I don't think he's in.'

'There's a light in his studio,' she pointed out. 'So he must be. Here!' She slipped a note into his hand and hurried past him to the stairs. He stared at the note and shuffled back into his flat.

'You?' said Arnold Palfy, as he opened the door upstairs.

'Right first time,' answered Irene Gerlach sourly, and walked into the studio. She sat down, lit a cigarette, and looked at him expectantly.

He said nothing.

'Why did you refuse to speak to me on the telephone?' she asked. 'Do you think it very civil?'

'I didn't refuse to speak to you.'

'Didn't you?'

'I wasn't capable of speaking. I didn't feel like it. The child was very ill.'

'But now she's better. Otherwise you would still be in Rotenturm Street.'

He nodded. 'Yes, she's better. And my wife is there.'

'Who?'

'My wife. My divorced wife. She arrived today with my other child.'

121

'Your *other* child!' echoed the fashionable young lady.

'Yes. They're twins. First Lisa was with me. But since the holidays it's been the other. And yet I didn't even notice it. I found out only yesterday.'

The lady laughed angrily. 'A bit of clever planning by your ex-wife!'

'She didn't find out till yesterday herself,' he said impatiently.

Irene Gerlach curled her pretty painted lips ironically. 'The situation has some piquancy, hasn't it? In one flat is a woman you used to be married to, and in the other a woman you're not married to yet.'

His temper rose. 'There are plenty of other flats and plenty of other women I'm not married to.'

'Oh! You can be witty too, can you?'

'I'm sorry, Irene. My nerves are on edge.'

'I'm sorry, Arnold. So are mine.'

Bang! The door was shut and Miss Gerlach was outside it.

Mr Palfy stared for some time at the closed door, then he strolled over to the piano, looked through the pages of music-paper covered with notes of his children's opera, took out one page, and sat down at the keyboard.

For a time he played from his notes. A simple, severe canon in one of the modes of old church music. Then he began to modulate. From the Dorian to C minor, from C minor to E major. And slowly, quite slowly, a new melody budded out of the paraphrase. A tune so simple and winsome that it might have been sung by two little girls with pure, clear, childish

A summer meadow, by a cool mountain lake

voices; in a summer meadow, by a cool mountain lake
that mirrored the blue heaven: the heaven that is
high above our understanding, whence shines the
sun, warming all creatures, without distinction of
good, bad, or indifferent.

Chapter 11

IT is proverbial that time heals wounds, but it also cures sickness. Lottie was well again, and once more she was wearing her plaits and ribbons. And Lisa had her curls again and could shake them to her heart's content.

They helped their mother and Rosa with the shopping and the housework. They played in the nursery. They sang duets while Lottie – and sometimes even Daddy – played the piano. They called on Mr Gabel in the flat next door. Or they took Peterkin for walks, while Dr Strobel was busy with his patients. Peterkin had adjusted himself to the two-fold Lisa, first by doubling his capacity for loving little girls and then by halving it. He had to find a solution somehow.

But sometimes the sisters looked apprehensively into each other's eyes. What was to happen now?

*

On the 14th October they both had their birthday. They were sitting with their parents in the nursery. Two circles of candles had been lighted, each with ten candles. There had been home-made cakes and cups of steaming chocolate. Daddy had played a wonderful 'Birthday March for Twins'. Now he swung round on the piano-stool and said, 'Tell me why you wouldn't let us give you presents.'

Lottie took a deep breath and answered, 'Because we want something you can't buy.'

'What is it you want, darling?' asked Mummy.

Now it was Lisa's turn to take a deep breath. Then she explained, jigging about with excitement. 'The present Lottie and I want for our birthday is to be able to live together always.' It was out at last.

Their parents said nothing.

Lottie added very softly. 'Then you needn't ever give us a present again as long as we live! Not for birthdays and not for Christmas. Never at all!'

Mummy and Daddy still said nothing.

'You might try it, anyway.' Lisa had tears in her eyes. 'We'll behave ever so well. A lot better than we do at present. And everything will be a lot, lot better.'

Lottie nodded. 'We promise!'

'Word of honour and cross our hearts!' added Lisa quickly.

Their father got up from the piano-stool. 'If you

agree, Lisalotte, I think we'll have a word in the next room.'

'Yes, Arnold,' replied his ex-wife. And then the two of them went into the next room, and the door closed behind them.

'Cross your fingers!' whispered Lisa excitedly. Eight small fingers were crossed and four small thumbs clenched tight.

Lottie moved her lips silently.

'Are you saying a prayer?' asked Lisa.

Lottie nodded.

Then Lisa's lips began to move also. 'For what we are about to receive may the Lord make us truly thankful,' she murmured half to herself.

Lottie shook her plaits reprovingly.

'I know it's out of place,' whispered Lisa, a little abashed. 'But it's all I can think of. For what we are about to receive may the Lord –'

'Putting our own position on one side,' Mr Palfy was just saying in the next room, staring fixedly at the floor, 'there's no doubt it would be much better for the children if they stayed together.'

'Of course,' said the young woman. 'We ought never to have parted them.'

Mr Palfy was still looking hard at the floor. 'We have a lot to make up for.' He cleared his throat. 'Well, I agree to your – to your taking both children back to Munich.'

She put her hand to her heart.

'Perhaps,' he went on, 'you'll let them come and stay with me for four weeks every year?'

She did not answer, so he went on, 'Or three

weeks? Or at least a fortnight? I don't suppose you believe me, but I'm really very fond of them both.'

'Why shouldn't I believe you?' he heard her say.

He shrugged his shoulders. 'I have not given much proof of it.'

'Yes, you have – at Lottie's sick bed,' she answered. 'But how do you know that they would be as happy as we wish them to be, if they grow up without a father?'

'They certainly couldn't grow up without you.'

'Oh, Arnold. Don't you really see what they want, though they didn't dare say it?'

'Of course I do.' He went to the window. 'Of course I know what they want.' He tugged impatiently at the window-catch. 'They want you and me to stay together.'

'They want a father *and* a mother – our twins! Is that selfish of them?' asked the young woman eagerly.

'No, but wishes need not be selfish to be unattainable.' He stood by the window like a little boy, who has been stood in the corner and defiantly refuses to come out of it.

'Why is it unattainable?'

He turned in surprise. 'You ask *me* that? After all that's happened?'

She looked at him earnestly and gave a scarcely perceptible nod. Then she said, 'Yes. After all that's happened!'

Lisa was standing by the door, one eye glued to the keyhole. Lottie was at her side, both hands spread out, the fingers crossed.

'Oh, oh, oh!' cried Lisa. 'Daddy's giving Mummy a kiss!'

Quite contrary to her usual custom, Lottie pushed her sister roughly aside and peered through the keyhole.

'Well?' asked Lisa. 'Is he still doing it?'

'No,' whispered Lottie, standing up with a radiant smile. 'Now Mummy's giving Daddy a kiss.'

Then the twins hooted with glee and fell into each other's arms.

Chapter 12

MR BENNO PREISS, the experienced registrar of the first district of Vienna, was performing a marriage which, in spite of all his experience, caused him occasional twinges of misgiving. The bride was the divorced wife of the bridegroom. The two terrifyingly similar ten-year-old girls were the daughters of the happy couple. The one witness, an artist, Anton Gabel by name, was not wearing a tie. But, just to even things up, the other witness, a certain Dr Strobel, had brought a dog. And the dog made such a commotion in the vestibule, where it ought to have been left, that it had to be brought in and allowed to take part in the ceremony. A dog as witness at a wedding! Really, what were things coming to!

Lottie and Lisa sat reverently on their chairs and were as happy as princesses. And they were not only

Mr Benno Preiss was performing a marriage

happy but proud, very proud indeed. For all this marvellous, unbelievable happiness had been brought about by them. What would have happened to their poor parents if it had not been for the children?

Well, then. And it had not been easy either to keep one's mouth shut and play the role of fate. Adventures, tears, anxiety, deception, despair, illness – nothing had been spared them. Not a thing!

After the ceremony Mr Gabel whispered to Mr Palfy and the two men, each with his artistic temperament, twinkled mysteriously at each other. But why they whispered and twinkled no one knew except themselves.

All that Mrs Horn – formerly Palfy and now Palfy for the second time – had heard her ex- and present husband say, was 'Too early?' Then he turned to her and went on fluently, 'I've got an idea. Do you know what? We'll drive round to the school and register Lottie.'

'Lottie! But Lottie's been there for – Oh yes, of course. You're quite right.'

Mr Palfy gave Mrs Palfy a tender look. 'I should say so indeed.'

*

Mr Kilian, headmaster of the girls' school, was genuinely flabbergasted when Mr Palfy and his wife registered a second daughter, who appeared to be quite identical with the first. But, as an old schoolmaster, he had had many experiences no less remarkable, and so he soon recovered his balance.

When the new pupil had been officially entered in

the big register, he leaned back comfortably in his desk-chair. 'As a young assistant teacher,' he said, 'I once had an experience about which I should like to tell you. One Easter a new boy came to the school. He came from a poor home but he was as clean as a pink and, as I soon found, very keen on his work. He made good progress. In arithmetic he was soon the best in the class. But he varied! For some time I was mystified. Then I thought, "This is most extraordinary – sometimes he does his sums like a calculating machine, without a single mistake. At other times he is much slower, and much less accurate."'

The headmaster paused for effect, and his eyes twinkled benevolently at Lisa and Lottie. 'At last I hit on the following plan: I noted down in a book the days when the boy did his arithmetic well and the days when he did it badly. And my plan produced a very strange result: on Mondays, Wednesdays, and Fridays he was good, on Tuesdays, Thursdays, and Saturdays he was bad.'

'Think of that!' said Mr Palfy. And the two little girls fidgeted on their chairs.

'I went on making these notes for six weeks,' continued the old gentleman. 'It never altered. Mondays, Wednesdays, and Fridays, good. Tuesdays, Thursdays, and Saturdays, bad. So one fine day I went round to his parents' home and informed them of my puzzling observation. They looked at each other, half embarrassed, half amused, and then the husband said, "What you say is about right, sir." Then he whistled on two fingers, and two boys came running in from the next room. *Two*. The same height.

132

the same looks in every respect. "They're twins," said the wife. "Sepp is good at arithmetic and Toni is – the other one." When I recovered a little, I said, "But tell me, why don't you send both boys to school?" And the father answered, "We're poor, sir. The two boys have only one good suit between them."'

The Palfys laughed. Mr Kilian beamed, and Lisa cried, 'That's an idea! We'll do the same!'

'You just dare!' said Mr Kilian, threatening her with his finger. 'Oh dear, no. Miss Gestettner and Miss Bruckbaur will have enough trouble without that!'

'Especially,' said Lisa, carried away, 'if we do our hair the same way and change places.'

The headmaster clapped his hands above his head and gave other signs of being on the verge of desperation. 'Terrible!' he cried. 'And what's to happen later on, when you are young women and someone wants to marry you?'

'Since we look the same,' said Lottie thoughtfully, 'we're sure to have the same man fall in love with us both.'

'And we're sure both to fall in love with the same man,' cried Lisa. 'Then we shall both have to marry him. That's the best way. Mondays, Wednesdays, and Fridays I shall be his wife. And Tuesdays, Thursdays, and Saturdays it will be Lottie's turn.'

'And if he doesn't happen to try you out at arithmetic,' said Mr Palfy laughing, 'he'll never notice that he has two wives instead of one.'

Mr Kilian got up from his chair. 'Poor fellow,' he remarked pityingly.

Mrs Palfy smiled. 'But there'll be one good thing about it – he'll have a day off on Sundays!'

*

As the newly-wed, or, more precisely, the newly *re-*wed parents crossed the playground with the twins, morning break had just begun. Hundreds of little girls elbowed and were elbowed in their turn, as they stared incredulously at Lisa and Lottie.

At last Trudie succeeded in fighting her way through as far as the twins. Panting for breath, she looked from one to the other. Her first words were, 'I say!' Then she turned with an injured expression to Lisa. 'First you make me promise not to say a word about it at school, and then the two of you come here as bold as brass!'

'It was I who made you promise,' corrected Lottie.

'Now you can go ahead and tell everybody,' said Lisa graciously. 'Tomorrow morning we're both coming.'

Then Mr Palfy forced his way through the crowd like an ice-breaker, and piloted his family to the school-gates. Trudie meanwhile became the victim of her school-fellows' curiosity. They bunted her up on to the branch of a rowan tree, whence she told everything she knew to the listening crowd of girls.

The bell rang. Break was over. Or so you would have thought.

The mistresses went back to the classrooms. The classrooms were empty. The mistresses went to the windows and looked down with shocked expressions into the playground. The playground was packed.

134

The mistresses crowded into the headmaster's room to chorus their complaints.

'Sit down, ladies,' he said. 'The porter has just brought me the current number of the *Munich Illustrated*. The front page is of great interest to this school. Would you mind reading it, Miss Bruckbaur?' He handed her the paper.

And now the teachers too forgot – just like the girls in the playground – that break was long since over.

*

Miss Irene Gerlach, smartly dressed as ever, was standing outside the Opera House, looking with astonishment at the front page of the *Munich Illustrated*, on which appeared a photograph of two little girls in plaits. When she looked up her expression grew more astonished than ever. For a taxi had just stopped at the crossing and in the taxi were two little girls with a gentleman whom she had once known well and a lady whom she hoped never to know at all.

Lottie nudged her sister. 'Look over there!'

'Ah-uh! What is it?'

Lottie whispered, so softly that the words could scarcely be heard, 'Miss Gerlach!'

'Where?'

'On the right. The one with a big hat and a paper in her hand.' Lisa peered across at the fashionable lady. She would have liked to put out her tongue at her.

'What are you two up to?'

Goodness, now Mummy had probably noticed something!

But by good luck a distinguished old lady leaned

out of a car that was waiting next to the taxi. She offered Mummy an illustrated paper, and said, smiling, 'I think this might interest you.'

Mrs Palfy took the paper, looked at the front page, nodded and smiled, and passed it to her husband.

The cars began to move. The old lady nodded graciously.

The children climbed up on the seat beside Daddy, and inspected the photograph on the front page.

'That Mr Appeldauer!' cried Lisa. 'Fancy him letting us down like that!'

'And we thought we'd torn up *all* the prints,' said Lottie.

'But he still had the plates,' explained Mummy. 'So he could take hundreds of prints from them.'

'What a good thing he did let you down,' said Daddy. 'If he hadn't, Mummy would never have discovered your secret, and then there would have been no wedding.'

Lisa squirmed suddenly round and looked back at the Opera House. But far and wide there was no sign of Miss Gerlach.

Lottie said to her mother, 'We'll write a letter of thanks to Mr Appeldauer.'

*

The 'newly-weds' and the twins climbed the stairs of the house in Rotenturm Street.

Rosa in her best dress was waiting at the open door, smiling across the whole breadth of her peasant face. She handed the bride a big bunch of flowers.

'Thank you very much, Rosa,' returned Mrs Palfy. 'And I'm glad you've decided to stay with us.'

Rosa nodded as vigorously and jerkily as a puppet in a Punch and Judy show. Then she stammered, 'I ought to go back to the farm. To my father. But, you see, I'm so fond of Miss Lottie.'

Conductor Palfy laughed. 'That's not very polite to the other three of us, Rosa.'

Not knowing what to say, Rosa shrugged her shoulders.

Mrs Palfy came to the rescue. 'Well, we can't stand at the door for ever.'

'Sorry, madam!' Rosa made way for them to pass.

'Just a second,' said Mr Palfy, with a broad grin. 'I must just slip across to the other flat.'

The rest of the party froze. Surely he would not go back to his studio in Ring Street on his wedding-day! (No, Rosa had not frozen, not a bit of it! She was laughing up her sleeve.)

Mr Palfy went to the door of Mr Gabel's flat, took out a key, and calmly unlocked it!

Lottie ran to him. On the door was a new nameplate, and on the new name-plate was clearly engraved the one word, 'Palfy'.

'Oh, Daddy!' she cried blissfully.

And then Lisa was at her side. She read the nameplate, grabbed her sister by the collar, and began to execute a sort of St Vitus's dance. The old stairway shook at every joint.

'That's enough,' cried Mr Palfy at last. 'Off you go to the kitchen and help Rosa.' He looked at his watch. 'I'm just going to show Mummy my studio-flat, and in half an hour we'll have lunch. So when it's ready just ring the bell.' He took their mother by the hand.

In the opposite doorway Lisa dropped a curtsey. 'I hope we shall be good neighbours, Mr Palfy.'

*

The young woman took off her hat and coat. 'What a surprise!' she said softly.

'A pleasant surprise?' he asked.

She nodded.

'It was Lottie's wish for some time before it was mine,' he said slowly. 'Gabel worked out every detail of the plan of campaign and directed the battle of the furniture vans.'

'So that is why we had to call at the school?'

'Yes. Moving the grand piano gave the all-in furniture wrestlers a spot of bother.'

They went into his workroom. Resurrected from the drawer of his desk, the photograph of a young woman that dated from a past but unforgotten time, stood on his piano. He put his arm round her. 'On the third floor left, all four of us will be happy together, and on the third floor right, I shall be happy alone. But only on the other side of the wall.'

'So much happiness!' She nestled against him.

'Anyhow, more than we deserve,' he said seriously. 'But not more than we can bear.'

'I should never have believed it possible.'

'What?'

'That one can make up for lost happiness, like a lesson one has missed at school.'

He pointed to a picture on the wall. A small, earnest, childish face, as Gabel had drawn it, looked down from its frame at the two parents, 'We owe every second of our new happiness,' he said, 'to our two children.'

*

Lisa, decked in a kitchen apron, was standing on a chair, fastening to the wall with drawing-pins the front page of the *Munich Illustrated*.

'Beautiful!' said Rosa, almost reverently.

Lottie, also in a kitchen apron, was pottering about at the stove.

Rosa dabbed a tear from the corner of her eye, sniffed gently, and asked, still standing in front of the picture, 'Which of you two is really which?'

The two girls looked at each other, startled. Then they looked at the picture pinned on the wall, and then at each other again.

'Well,' began Lottie doubtfully.

'When Mr Appeldauer took us, I think I was on the right,' said Lisa, trying to remember.

Lottie shook her head slowly. 'No, I was on the right ... Or was I?'

The two girls craned their necks and stared at their portrait.

'Well, if you yourselves don't know which is which –' cried Rosa, completely nonplussed, and began to laugh.

'No. We ourselves don't know!' shouted Lisa, tickled to death. And then all three were laughing so loudly that the noise could be heard in the flat next door.

And Mrs Palfy asked, almost frightened, 'Will you be able to work in a noise like that?'

He went to the piano and said, as he opened it, 'Only in a noise like that!' And as the laughter next door died down, he played his wife the duet in E sharp from the Children's Opera, and Rosa and the twins heard it and worked as quietly as mice so as not to miss a single note.

When the song was over Lottie asked shyly, 'What's going to happen now, Rosa? Since Daddy and Mummy are both back here with us, do you think Lisa and I may have some brothers and sisters?'

'Of course,' declared Rosa confidently. 'Do you want them?'

'I should say we do,' answered Lisa emphatically.

'Boys or girls?' asked Rosa.

'Boys *and* girls,' said Lottie.

But Lisa cried from the bottom of her heart, 'And twins every time!'

More Books from Puffin

JELLYBEAN *Tessa Duder*

A sensitive modern novel about Geraldine, alias 'Jellybean', who leads a rather solitary life as the only child of a single parent. She's tired of having to fit in with her mother's busy schedule, but a new friend and a performance of 'The Nutcracker Suite' change everything.

THE PRIESTS OF FERRIS *Maurice Gee*

Susan Ferris and her cousin Nick return to the world of O which they had saved from the evil Halfmen, only to find that O is now ruled by cruel and ruthless priests. Can they save the inhabitants of O from tyranny? An action-packed and gripping story by the author of prize-winning THE HALFMEN OF O.

THE SEA IS SINGING *Rosalind Kerven*

In her seaside Shetland home, Tess is torn between the plight of the whales and loyalty to her father and his job on the oil rig. A haunting and thought-provoking novel.

BACK HOME *Michelle Magorian*

A marvellously gripping story of an irrepressible girl's struggle to adjust to a new life. Twelve-year-old Rusty, who had been evacuated to the United States when she was seven, returns to the grey austerity of post-war Britain.

THE OUTSIDE CHILD *Nina Bawden*

Imagine suddenly discovering you have a step-brother and -sister no one has ever told you about! It's the most exciting thing that's ever happened to Jane, and she can't wait to meet them. Perhaps at last she will become part of a 'proper' family, instead of forever being the outside child. So begins a long search for her brother and sister, but when she finally does track them down, Jane finds there are still more surprises in store!

THE FOX OF SKELLAND *Rachel Dixon*

Samantha's never liked the old custom of Foxing Day – the fox costume especially gives her the creeps. So when Jason and Rib, children of the new publicans at The Fox and Lady, find the costume and Jason wears it to the fancy-dress disco, she's sure something awful will happen.

Then Sam's old friend Joseph sees the ghost of the Lady and her fox. Has she really come back to exact vengeance on the village? Or has her appearance got something to do with the spate of burglaries in the area?

ASTERCOTE *Penelope Lively*

Astercote village was destroyed by plague in the fourteenth century and Mair and her brother Peter find themselves caught up in a strange adventure when an ancient superstition is resurrected.

THE HOUNDS OF THE MÓRRIGAN *Pat O'Shea*

When the Great Queen Mórrigan, evil creature from the world of Irish mythology, returns to destroy the world, Pidge and Brigit are the children chosen to thwart her. How they go about it makes an hilarious, moving story, full of original and unforgettable characters.

NICOBOBINUS *Terry Jones*

Nicobobinus and his friend, Rosie, find themselves in all sorts of intriguing adventures when they set out to find the Land of the Dragons long ago. Stunningly illustrated by Michael Foreman.

FRYING AS USUAL *Joan Lingard*

When Mr Francetti breaks his leg it looks as if his fish restaurant will have to close so Toni, Rosita and Paula decide to keep things going.

DRIFT *William Mayne*

A thrilling adventure of a young boy and an Indian girl, stranded on a frozen floating island in the North American wilderness.

MIGHTIER THAN THE SWORD *Clare Bevan*

Adam had always felt he was somehow special, different from the rest of the family, but could he really be a modern-day King Arthur, the legendary figure they're learning about at school? Inspired by the stories they are hearing in class, Adam and his friends become absorbed in a complex game of knights and good deeds. All they need is a worthy cause for which to fight. So when they discover that the local pond is under threat, Adam's knights are ready to join battle with the developers.

Reality and legend begin to blur in this lively, original story about an imaginative boy who doesn't let a mere wheelchair get in his way of adventure.